MY KIND OF TOWN

SHELLY LAURENSTON

My Kind of Town

Cover design by Cynthia Lucas.

ISBN: 978-1-68068-192-5

This book is published on behalf of the author by the Ethan Ellenberg Literary Agency.

You can reach the author at:
Facebook: https://www.facebook.com/ShelLaurenston/
Website: www.shellylaurenston.com

MY KIND OF TOWN

Emma Luchessi may be a witch from Long Island but she is used to her life being quiet. Some may even say boring. She doesn't mind boring. Boring is safe. Calm. Peaceful. Like beige. One doesn't get into trouble with beige. But a wrong turn off a southern highway is about to turn Emma's beige life into everything *but* boring.

Kyle Treharne's a good ol' boy with a sheriff's badge and a difficult population to manage. He wishes he had to worry about gangs and drugs and carjackings. Instead, he has to worry about big cats fighting with wolves, bears fighting over honey, and hyenas fighting with everyone. And now, out of nowhere, he's got a human outsider riling up all the locals by asking too many questions. She's just so paranoid. And doesn't trust Kyle a lick. These city gals. They just don't know how to relax, do they?

Of course, Kyle is a big cat. He knows how to relax and he'd be more than willing to help Emma learn how. He'd be willing to help Emma do all sorts of things if she'd just give him half a chance.

But it turns out Emma coming to Smithville isn't a simple accident. She's been brought here and she's bringing change and danger right along with her. Lucky for Emma, Kyle and the rest of the town like a bit of danger...

Even if they don't feel the same way about city folk.

TABLE OF CONTENTS

ONE

"There's blood everywhere."

Kyle Treharne leaned into the passenger side of the overturned car, the driver's side so badly damaged no one could get through the crumpled metal to extract themselves. Not even the female whose fear he could smell. Her fear and panic...and something else. Something he couldn't quite name.

"Do you see anybody?" his boss asked. Kyle readjusted the earplug to hear the man better. The sheriff's voice was so low, it was often hard to make out exactly what he'd said.

"Nope. I don't see anyone. No bodies, but..." He sniffed the air and looked down. "Blood trail."

"Follow it. Let me know what you find. I'll send out the EMS guys."

"You got it." Kyle disconnected and followed the trail of blood heading straight toward the beach. He moved fast, worried the woman might be bleeding to death, but also concerned this human female would see something he'd never be able to explain.

Kyle pushed through the trees until he hit the beach. As he'd hoped, none of the town's people or resort visitors were hanging around, the beach thankfully deserted in the middle of this hot August day. He followed the blood, cutting in a small arc across the sand, the trail leading back into the woods about twenty feet from where he'd entered.

He'd barely gone five feet when a bright flash of light and the missing woman's scent hit him hard, seconds before *she* hit him hard. He should have been faster. Normally, he would be. That scent of hers, though, threw him completely off balance, and he couldn't snap out of it quick enough to avoid the woman slamming right into him.

Her body hit his so hard that if he were completely human, she might have killed him.

But Kyle wasn't human. He'd been born different, like nearly everyone else in his small town. They might not all be the same breed, but they were all the same *kind*.

Still, his less-than-human nature didn't mean he didn't experience pain. At the moment, he felt lots and lots of pain as he landed flat on his back, the woman on top of him.

Yet the pain faded away when the woman moved, her small body brushing against his. She moaned and Kyle reached around to gently grip her shoulders.

"Hey, darlin'. You all right?"

She didn't answer. Instead, she slapped her hand over his face, squashing his nose. Putting all her weight on that hand, she pushed herself up.

Between her fingers, he could see the confusion in her eyes as she looked around. Blood from a deep gash on her forehead matted her dark brown hair and covered part of her face. Bloodshot, dark-brown eyes searched the area. For what, Kyle had no idea. A cut slashed across her top lip, and although it no longer bled, it had started to turn the area around it black and blue.

Damn, little girl is cute.

"Uh…" He tapped her arm. "Could you move your hand, sweetheart?" The question came out like he had the worst cold in the universe. "I can't really breathe."

She didn't even look at him, instead staring off into the forest. "Dammit. It's gone." Putting more pressure on his poor nose, the woman levered herself up and off him. "Damn. Damn. Damn." She stumbled toward the forest, and Kyle quickly got to his feet.

"This isn't my fault. It's not," the woman blurted.

Poor thing, completely delirious from all that blood loss and muttering to herself like a mental patient, Kyle thought.

Then she stopped walking. Abruptly. Almost as if she'd walked into a wall. "Damn," she said again.

Knowing he had to get her to the hospital before she died on him, Kyle put his hand on her shoulder, gently turning her so she could see him. "It's all right, darlin'. Let's get you out of here, okay?" He slipped one arm behind her back and the other under her knees, scooping her up in his arms.

Hmm. She feels nice there.

Kyle smiled down at her and, for a moment, she looked at him in complete confusion.

Then the crazy woman started swinging and kicking, trying to get out of his arms. Although she had no skills—she did little more than flail wildly—he couldn't believe her strength with all the blood she'd lost, but he quickly realized someone else had caught on to her scent, too, and was heading right for them.

Kyle gripped the fighting woman around the waist, dragging her back against him with one arm. Ignoring how much her tiny fists and feet were starting to hurt, he turned his body so she faced in the opposite direction and with his free hand, swung up and back, slamming the back of his fist into the muzzle of the black and orange striped Yankee bastard hellbent on getting his tiger paws on the woman in Kyle's arms. Tiger males only had to get a whiff of a female and they were on them like white on rice. The fact that this

3

SHELLY LAURENSTON

woman was full human and an outsider didn't seem to matter to some idiots.

A surprised yelp and the Yankee cat flipped back into the woods. Kyle rolled his eyes. He loved his town but, Lord knew, he didn't like the Yankees who often came to call. All of them rude, pretentious, and damn annoying.

Kyle walked off with the woman still trapped in his arm until she started slapping at him.

"Hands off! Hands off! Let me go!" After all that blood loss, she seemed completely lucid but quite insane.

Even worse...he'd recognize that accent anywhere. A Yankee. A *damn* Yankee.

Kyle dropped her on her cute butt, and she slammed hard into the sand.

After a moment of stunned silence, she suddenly glared up at him with those big brown eyes...and just like that, Kyle Treharne knew he was in the biggest trouble of his life.

No, no. *That* was not a normal-size human being. Not by a long shot. Her Coven had warned her, "They grow 'em big in the South, sweetie," but she had no idea they grew *this* big.

Nor this gorgeous. She'd never seen hair that black before. Not brown. Black. But when the sunlight hit it in the right way, she could see other colors *under* the black. Light shades of red and yellow and brown. Then there were his eyes. Light, *light* gold eyes flickered over her face, taking in every detail. His nose, blunt at the tip; his lips full and quite lickable.

"You gonna calm down now, darlin'? Or should I drop you on that pretty ass again?"

Emma Lucchesi—worshipper of the Dark Mothers, power elemental of the Coven of the Darkest Night,

4

ninth-level master of the dream realm, and Long Island accountant for the law offices of Bruce, MacArthur, and Markowitz—didn't know what to say to that. What to say to *him*. Mostly because she couldn't stop staring at the man standing over her.

Routine. This should have been routine. A simple search for a power source, necessary so they didn't have to worry about blood sacrifices. Their last two power sources had dried up fast. Faster than usual, so they'd gone searching outside of their hometown. They simply didn't mean to go *this* outside their hometown. And somehow the Coven had opened a doorway they now had to scramble to close. Leaving dimensional doors open for too long led to all sorts of problems.

Using a few location spells and some powerful runes the Coven possessed, Emma had located the spot somewhere on the coast in the Carolinas. Normally, Emma's role simply involved her finding out the where, and someone else in the Coven would solve the problem.

Just as at her day job, Emma handled the minutiae. The details. The little things. Someone else handled the more dramatic or interesting things. And this time would have been no different if it hadn't been for one little problem...

"North Carolina? In the South? Oh. Um. Well, you know, I really shouldn't take any more time off work." If she'd said London or Paris or even San Francisco or Chicago, there would have been a full-on screaming match about who should go or not go. Even her high priestess, Jamie Meacham, would have had to at least go toe to toe with her cousin, Mackenzie Mathews.

So, in the end, Emma ended up trapped on this little excursion because no one else wanted to head on down South to take care of such a minor situation.

Of course, Emma still wasn't quite clear how her "minor situation" went into full-blown catastrophe in seconds. One moment she was typically lost, unable to find the town called Smithville anywhere on any of her AAA maps although a giant "Welcome" billboard told her that was exactly where she was. Then, like a stray dog, it came out of nowhere, stepping right in front of her beige rental car. She could have stopped in time but, unlike a stray dog, it charged her. Head on. Slamming into the hood of her car and crumpling it around her. Trapping her. And killing her if she hadn't moved quickly. As the metal buckled and screamed around her, she called to her sisters. Called to them and took their power, yanking it clean and surrounding herself with it. Letting the power of the Dark Mothers flow through her.

She woke up outside the crumpled remains of her rental car with no idea how she got there, lying in a pool of her own blood. Yet she could feel her strength returning, feel the protective power of her Coven healing open wounds and reviving dwindling blood.

Her body still needed to heal completely, though, because while the doorway had been closed—sending her careening into this gigantic malcontent—the thing that had tried to kill her still ran loose. She had to get to that thing before it killed someone. She didn't know if her Coven had unleashed it when they opened that doorway, but she sure as hell couldn't leave it to go wandering around some dinky little Southern town like in some horror movie.

Swallowing hard, Emma forced words out of her throat. "I need to go." It was the most she could manage at the moment as her insides repaired themselves.

"Yup. You sure do." He crouched in front of her, and she silently sighed in relief when she finally saw the Smithville County Sheriff's Department logo on his T-shirt. Originally all she saw was a beautiful man in black jeans, black boots, and a perfectly fitted black T-shirt. Black in the middle of August didn't make sense to her, but he did look good.

One of his big hands reached out, and she immediately reared back. He blinked in surprise and said, "Don't worry, darlin'. No one's gonna hurt you. I just need to look at your head. And then we need to get you to the hospital."

"No," she forced out, sounding way tougher than she felt. "No hospital."

He grinned and she felt her skin tingle.

"I love how you think you've got some say here, darlin'."

Big strong hands that could probably wring her chicken neck, gently lifted her hair off her face. She frowned deeply, not because he touched her, but because he might notice exactly how quickly the cut on her head was healing. Hell of a lot faster than it should.

She slapped at his hand. "Stop touching me!"

When he sighed, she wasn't sure why he sounded so exasperated. Weren't cops trained to deal with difficult victims? Jamie and Mac had been. A cop and a firefighter, respectively, the two of them could handle most situations Emma and the rest of the Coven would run screaming from.

"Are you going to keep being this difficult?"

"Yes," she said simply.

"Fine, then." Without another word, he put his arms around her, lifting her up as he stood.

"Wha...what are you doing?"

"Taking you to my truck so I can get you to the hospital. I don't want to wait any more for EMS. And stop wiggling, woman." She didn't, but he pulled her closer into his body. "What did I just say?"

She glared at him, unable to say another word.

"Oh, good. You can follow orders."

Son of a—

"And don't curse at me in your head." Freakishly light gold eyes stared down into her face. She'd never seen eyes that color before in her life. "'Cause I know you are."

She rolled her eyes and he raised one coal-black eyebrow. After nearly a minute of mutual silent staring, he nodded and walked on and Emma sulked.

Sulked because she was simply too weak to fight anymore. Between the blood loss and what she'd already done to close the door, she could barely keep her eyes open. In fact, maybe a little nap would—

"Oh, no you don't. I need you awake, darlin'."

Sighing, she forced her eyes open. "Stop calling me darling."

He chuckled and pulled her tighter into his wonderfully warm body. "Fine, then. I'll call you exactly what you are…"

Emma waited for it. If she were home, she knew exactly what he'd call her. What she'd been called before when she ignored a strange drunk guy on the street or when she didn't step off the gas fast enough at a changing light. But the next word out of his mouth had her stiffening in his arms.

"Yankee."

And what bothered her most was how disgusted he sounded.

TWO

"You do know she should be dead, right?"

Kyle nodded. "Yeah. I know."

Dr. Dale Sahara, a Harvard-trained physician whose head Kyle had dunked in a toilet when he found out the big-haired bastard had been messing with his baby sister, removed his latex gloves. "And yet, she seems to be healing quite quickly."

"How quickly?"

The big man shrugged and tossed his gloves into a bright red trash can. "I only had to put two stitches in her forehead, and her lip didn't even need a Band-Aid once I wiped off all the blood."

"How is that possible? There was blood all over her car. All over her. And her car's totaled."

"I understand that. I'm simply telling you what I saw once I cleaned her up."

"What about internal damage?"

A sudden tic started in Sahara's jaw, and Kyle knew he'd asked the pompous bastard one too many questions. Good. He hadn't liked Dale Sahara in high school, and he sure didn't like him now.

"You don't think I checked for that?" Sahara snapped.

Kyle gave a casual shrug. "Just making sure you're paying attention, Doc. You know, doing your job."

The man's hand curled into a fist, but he still seemed to keep control. Although, Kyle had to admit, he did love messing with the man. The lions always made it so easy.

"All I know, Deputy, is that the woman is healing more quickly than seems normal."

"But she's not—"

Sahara didn't even let him finish. "No. She's full human."

"That's what I thought."

"Well, aren't you a smart alley cat."

Kyle's eyes narrowed. "Don't make me shove your head in the toilet again, Doc."

"I'd like to see you try," Sahara snarled, his fangs peeking out from under his lips.

Chucking his half-empty Coke can across the room and into the trash, Kyle walked over to Sahara, but one of the nurses stepped between them.

"Now, y'all cut that out right now. You're acting like a couple of dogs fightin' over some bone." She nodded at Kyle. "You better go check on her, Kyle. Your little human is gettin' awfully squirrelly. Keeps bitchin' her phone doesn't work and she wants to leave."

Kyle nodded. Her phone would never work around here. The town owned satellites to ensure it. "I'll handle it." He walked around the pair, heading back to the woman's room, but as he passed, he slapped the back of Sahara's big lion head with the palm of his hand.

And if the nurse hadn't grabbed the doc, holding on for dear life, that would have been one ugly fight.

Emma didn't get out much, she knew that. Admitted it openly. But when she did venture from her house, she was a watcher. That's what she did. She watched and she studied and she stared. But only when no one was looking.

Yet in all the years she'd stared at others, Emma had never seen so many good-looking people in one place before. The nurse…gorgeous. The doctor…gorgeous and so damn sweet. And that deputy guy…well, he went beyond gorgeous, but he was anything but sweet.

What disturbed her about him, though, was the fact that he kept staring at her, which really didn't make sense considering how gorgeous the nurses were. Except for the whole covered-in-blood thing, Emma should have been as invisible to these people as she was to everyone else in the world.

Emma, always a realist, wasn't perfect but a mutt—half Italian, half Chinese. Everyone gave her that look when she told them her last name, like they kept expecting it to end with "Ling" or "Chen." But other than that, Emma was nothing more than a nice girl from Long Island. An accountant who never cheated on her taxes although she knew how to work a buck, she held a nice, safe job in a big office building with many lawyers and accountants who didn't know she existed. She made decent money and didn't have any insane debts. She even drove a safe beige Toyota and lived a safe beige life. As one of her bitchy cousins once said, "You could make dull an Olympic sport."

No. Emma needed to get out of this town as soon as she could manage. It was giving her a complex. No one needed to be a Plain Jane in a land of beautiful people. That's why you'd never catch her in South Beach, Florida, or hanging out at some hot New York club. Nothing like having the pretty people ignore her.

Sliding off the bed, Emma grabbed her jeans. Probably once she got out of the hospital, her phone would work, too. She couldn't get a connection, and no one would give her a damn phone. She'd never been told no so many times in

her life, and always in the nicest way possible. She'd yet to
get one cross word from anybody.

Emma struggled into her jeans, pulling them up under
her way-too-big hospital gown. Frowning, she reached for
her blood-covered T-shirt. She'd rather not put it on, but
she didn't have much choice. So, grabbing the hospital
gown at the neck, she began to pull it down. She'd nearly
cleared her breasts when the words "What exactly are you
doing?" stopped her.

Holding the gown up against her, Emma spun around
and found the deputy standing there with his arms crossed
over his chest and his body leaning back against the door,
legs casually crossed at the ankles. Emma had the disturbing feeling he'd been standing there the entire time she'd
been busy putting her jeans on.

"You gonna answer me?" he drawled, his voice low, his
freaky light gold eyes sweeping up her body.

"No."

Chuckling, he stood up, arms and legs uncrossing. He
kind of unwound from the spot. Then he walked across the
room toward her, and Emma couldn't help but take a step
back, her eyes searching the room for another way out.

"Now, you're not going to try and get around me, are ya,
darlin'?"

If Emma were back in New York and some enormous
guy asked her that same question, she'd be screaming
"fire"—since screaming "help" or "rape" barely warranted
a raised eyebrow where she came from—and trying to dig
his eyes out. But something about this guy ... something she
couldn't quite understand had her frozen to the spot. Like
the time she got cornered by a pissed-off Rottweiller behind
her father's pizzeria. She'd known then if she made one
move it would go for her throat.

Frighteningly, this guy gave her the same nervous tic.

That big body stood over her, those light gold eyes staring into her face. "You insist on being difficult, don't you?" He took another step closer, and she could feel his body heat, smell his scent…and oh! But wasn't that nice.

Emma swallowed. "Difficult?"

"Yeah. Difficult." He took the T-shirt from her hand and tossed it back in the chair she'd originally left it in. "By trying to leave before the doc says it's okay." Those big fingers took firm hold of her hospital gown, and Emma suddenly stopped breathing as she waited to see what he'd do. Although she kind of knew what she'd like him to do…but that seemed wrong. She'd known this guy all of two seconds. She and her last boyfriend didn't start sharing a bed for three months after they started dating. When she mentioned this to her Coven during a casual dinner, they'd all simply stared at her, like she suddenly started speaking to them in Cantonese. So Emma didn't have sudden rushes of sexual passion—until now.

Gently, the deputy pried the gown from her fingers and slowly pulled it back onto her shoulders. His face completely impassive, he turned her, and she felt those fingers tie the gown back. She thought he'd stop there, then she gave a little squeak when she realized he'd crouched down behind her and grabbed hold of her jeans.

"Hold up!" She grabbed his hands through the gown. "What the hell do you think you're doing?"

"Just helping you out."

"I don't need your help," she yelped even as he pulled out of her grip and slipped her unzipped jeans back down, lifting each foot to remove the denim completely.

"There. Isn't that better?"

She turned around and glared at him, her face brutally hot. "No!"

He grinned at her and she almost smiled back. Almost.

"Now," he said while still crouching in front of her, dangerously near her pussy, "I don't want any more talk about you leavin'. You're staying until me and the doc say otherwise."

"What?" Panic. She was experiencing deep, bone-crushing panic. "You can't keep me if I don't want to stay."

"Oh, we sure can, darlin'. Ain't that right, Doc?"

Emma's head snapped up and, sure enough, the very gorgeous Dr. Sahara stood in the doorway, smiling at her. She got the feeling he'd been standing there the whole time the deputy had his way with her jeans. Did these people not make noise? Was this a Southern thing? Like grits and ham hocks?

"Now, Miss Emma," Dr. Sahara sweetly chastised, "we need to make sure you're okay before we let you go."

"You . . . you said I was okay. You said—"

"I said there was nothing obvious. But we'll want to keep you for observation. We wouldn't want something horrible to happen to you after you leave us. Would we, Deputy?"

"No. We want her safe and sound."

Emma looked down and realized that yes, the deputy had said that into her crotch. She'd never had this happen before. Standing so close to two men, rife with testosterone, who treated her like they thought she was hot. No one ever treated her like that, mostly because she blended into the woodwork. No one noticed Emma. They never had. And to be honest, she'd gotten quite used to it and preferred it that way.

She pushed past the man at her feet. "I appreciate your concern, gentlemen. But I really think—"

"This isn't up for debate, darlin'."

Emma stopped and turned to look at the deputy. The man took his time standing. That long body of his was one

14

big piece of rippling muscle, slowly unwinding to his full height. She almost moaned. She'd never seen a man so beautiful before. But there was something else about him. Something she couldn't quite put her finger on.

She did know one thing, though. He'd regret it if he made her get mean.

He'd regret it a lot.

One black eyebrow peaked as he stood in front of her, grinning down into her face. "Stop threatening me in your head. 'Cause we both know you are."

Emma didn't even want to know how the hell the man did that.

THREE

The last spoonful of imported Belgian chocolate pudding hovered near her mouth, her eyes were glued to the getting-odder-by-the-minute deputy. "What?"

"I asked how many brothers and sisters you have."

"Why?"

"Why what?"

"Why would you ask that?"

He blinked, staring at her like he didn't quite understand her. "Because that's polite conversation."

Maybe in the South, but where she came from it simply meant you were being nosy—and up to something.

"Are you going to answer me?"

Emma's eyes narrowed. "I have a few."

The deputy blinked again and then he sort of smiled. But it was definitely a "this girl is weirding me out" smile. "You have a few brothers and sisters? Your parents didn't give you a specific number?"

"They did. I'm simply not inclined to give it to you."

"Are you always this difficult to talk to?"

"Yes."

"Fine." He threw his hands up in frustration. "No more personal questions."

"Thank you."

She glanced at the Belgian pudding waiting to be eaten and realized she no longer wanted it. Carefully, Emma placed the spoon back on the tray, and the deputy stared at it.

"You gonna eat that?"

Emma scratched her head, avoiding any bumps or sore spots from the accident. "Uh...no."

Kyle grabbed the spoon covered in chocolate pudding, plopped it into his mouth, and, leaning back in his chair, casually sucked it clean. He did it so casually, she felt like they'd known each other for years. This should be where she went running for the hills. This should be where she contacted the state police to come rescue her from Insaneville, North Carolina.

Instead, for the first time in her life, all Emma wanted to do was jump into the man's lap, toss that spoon, and replace it with her tongue. She wanted him. She wanted a man who continually referred to her as "Yankee" or "darlin'."

No. No. It was time to go. Now. Before she made a complete and utter fool of herself in front of a bunch of beautiful people.

"I think in the morning I'll get another rental car and head to the airport in Wilmington. Head on home." That would give her the night to find her little "friend," kill it, and get that off her conscience before bailing this little freak town.

The deputy slowly pulled that spoon from his mouth, gave it a few extra swipes with his rather abnormally long tongue, smacked his lips, and said, "No."

Emma waited for more but it didn't come. "What do you mean...what do you mean no?"

He shrugged. Slowly, casually...annoyingly. "I mean no. You ain't goin' anywhere."

"You can't keep me here against my will."

"Why not?" He knew it was wrong, but he sure did enjoy watching her get all wound up and cranky when she didn't get what she wanted.

"What do you mean why not? It's against the law."

"I am the law, little gal," Kyle stated calmly, wishing she'd left him a little more of that pudding. For a hospital, they had the best food. But his kind, especially the snobby Prides, expected only the best, including imported chocolate pudding for their rare and usually brief hospital stays. "At least around here I am."

She stared at him for a moment, then she blinked and quickly looked away, doing anything and everything to avoid looking at him directly.

"I'm relatively certain," she ground out, her eyes focused across the room, "that's kidnapping."

"Not really." Kyle couldn't figure her out. She didn't seem scared of him, but she definitely didn't seem comfortable either. "It's for your own good. The doc said he didn't want you going anywhere until he was sure you were okay."

"For how long?"

Until I'm ready to let you go. "A few days."

Her eyes grew huge behind all that hair, and Kyle wanted nothing more than to comb that mess out of her face. By the time they moved her from emergency to her own room, she'd finger-combed all that hair in such a way he could barely see her gorgeous eyes. He hated it.

"A few days? I can't stay here a few days."

"Why? You told the doc you were on vacation. 'Just following where the sun leads' were your words, I believe. So what do you care if you stay here a few days or not?"

That seemed to stump her. "Uh..."

"Is that how you ended up in our little town, Emma? Following where the sun leads?"

She pushed her near-empty food tray away. "Yeah. Sure."

"Don't lie to me, Emma."

She glared at him through all that hair. "I'm not."

Kyle sighed. "Fine."

"I need to call my friends," she stated flatly. "I can't get a connection on my cell phone."

Her friends? Why not her family? Now that he thought about it, she hadn't said one word about her family. Most people, human or otherwise, wanted to see their family after an accident. Of course, she hadn't mentioned a boyfriend or husband either, which he found very comforting.

"Sure. I'll let you call your friends. As soon as you tell me why you're here."

"I'm on vacation."

"It's never a good idea to lie to the law, Miss Emma."

"It's never a good idea to hold someone against their will, Deputy. And yet, you don't seem to have a problem with that."

For someone who didn't give him much eye contact, she sure didn't back down easy. Standing, Kyle leaned over the metal rails of her hospital bed. "Let's try this again. Tell me why you're here."

She stared up at him, her eyes locked with his as she slowly crossed her arms under her chest. "I'm. On. Vacation."

Kyle nodded and stepped back. "All right, then. Hope you like this room. You'll be seeing it for quite a while."

"What does that mean?"

"It means until I get a straight answer from you, you're not going anywhere. So get comfortable."

He walked to the door. "I'll get some books and magazines from the shop to keep us entertained."

She didn't answer him, just turned her head and looked out the window.

❧   ❧   ❧

Emma closed the door of her hospital room bathroom. She groaned when she realized it didn't have a lock and knew she couldn't waste any time.

Flipping open the cell phone she'd snagged off the deputy's jeans when he'd been leaning over her and denying Emma her personal freedom, she quickly dialed a number and waited.

Her high priestess answered. "Meacham."

"Hey, Jamie. It's me."

"Em." The woman let out a deep, relieved breath. "You had me worried, girl."

"I had *you* worried?"

"But you're okay, right?"

"Yeah. I'm fine. In the hospital."

"Oh, sweetie—"

"No. No. Nothing like that. This local deputy found me and insisted on bringing me here. I think they're all a little freaked out I'm healing so fast. You wouldn't know anything about that would you, chief?"

Jamie gave a low chuckle. "Just trying to help."

When Emma had called on them, all she needed was their protection. Her body's sudden ability to quickly heal was merely Jamie showing off. "You helped, all right. Now they're suspicious as hell. And to be quite honest—"

"Yeah."

"These people are freaking me out. They're all so nice. But maybe a little *too* nice. And everyone is *huge*. Like, abnormally huge. And they're not on any maps. I mean, I searched every map, and nothing."

"What are you saying?"

"Two words. Government. Experiment."

20

"Did you hit your head a little hard on that steering wheel, hon?" Jamie asked. "Maybe crack your skull open?"

"I don't appreciate your sarcasm."

Jamie laughed. "Look, I warned you they were nice down there. And remember my cousins from Alabama? They're huge. They grow 'em big in the South. And most of those small podunk towns aren't on the maps."

"Podunk? What podunk town has Gucci, Versace, and Prada stores on its Main Street?"

"I don't know. Maybe they're like the Hamptons of North Carolina?"

"Then why won't they let me leave?"

"Whoa. Who won't?"

"The deputy and the doctor. They say I can't leave."

"Let me see if I understand. After a major car accident that should have killed you if it weren't for your Coven, but which still left you covered in blood, the doctor and the deputy won't let you leave the hospital? Those *bastards!*"

Emma gritted her teeth. "I'm hearing that sarcasm again."

Kyle picked up an issue of *Elle* magazine and debated whether Emma read this sort of stuff. She didn't seem real "fashion forward," as his baby sister called it. The jeans and T-shirt she had on when he found her were baggy and pretty boring. At the same time, she didn't seem like a scrub, either.

"Why can't you buy porn like the rest of us?"

Kyle sighed and didn't bother to turn around. "Why are you here?"

Tully Smith, his stepbrother and the mayor of Smithville, walked up to the magazine rack and grabbed a copy of *Architectural Digest*. It had been a dark day in Smithville when Kyle's daddy married Tully's momma. But Kyle and Tully had only been seven at the time and unable to prevent it, although they'd tried. Still, Kyle loved his momma more than he ever thought possible. From the first day, she never allowed the word "step" to be used in their home unless they were climbing some to go to their rooms. They were family, she'd say. No matter the differences. No matter the species.

"It's all over town some human crashed near the beach. And that you beat up one of our visitors."

"I didn't beat him up, I broke his nose. If I beat him up, there would have been lots more blood. Besides, he was charging her. I had to do something."

"I'm not arguing with you. I know how those big, dumb cats can be."

Kyle glared and Tully pretended to look appalled. "Of course I didn't mean you, little brother."

Three months apart, and the man insisted on calling him "little brother."

Grabbing a bunch of random magazines from the rack, Kyle headed toward the cashier. "You still haven't answered my question. Why are you here, canine?"

"I would like to meet our little visitor."

Not in this lifetime. Tully came from a long line of Alpha Males. Sometimes it seemed that's all the Smiths birthed. But in order to become the Alpha Male of any of the Smith Packs littered throughout the States, you had to have something the rest of the dogs didn't. Sure, they were all tough, strong, and pack oriented. But Tully was smart. Street smart. The kind of wolf that during a drought somehow always found water and food while other Packs were fighting over every drop and slowly starving to death. No way would Kyle let the conniving bastard near Emma.

"Forget it. She's recovering from the accident. I don't need you in there bothering her."

Tully followed him over to the counter. "Now, now, little pussy. No need to get all territorial. I'm only doing my job.

We both know it's strange she's here. And yet here she is. So the Elders want me to meet with her."

The Elders represented each Pride, Pack, Clan, and anything else lurking in their town. No matter their differences, they always worked together to protect the town.

"Right now my only concern is making sure she doesn't go wandering off. She seems real curious."

"The town's on high alert that a human's come to call. So you shouldn't be too worried. Doubt you'll see Randy Cartwright running down Main Street, giggling like an idiot while trying to bring down a bleeding antelope."

The brothers looked at each other and snorted out in unison, "Hyenas."

"Look, Emma, wait a day or two until they're sure you're okay, then come home."

"I can't. Not yet."

Jamie paused, then asked, "What aren't you telling me?"

Emma winced. "Nothing?"

"Emma..."

"Okay. Okay. Something, I think, tried to kill me. Maybe."

"This isn't that government-experiment theory again, is it?"

"No. Although I'm still right about that," she muttered.

"What was it?"

"It looked like a dog. An Old Schuck, maybe?"

"Have those even been seen in the last... I don't know... six hundred years?"

"I'm just telling you what I thought I saw. It looked like a big, shaggy Old Schuck."

"Are you safe? If someone's conjuring demon dogs from the pits of hell—"

"I'm fine," she answered quickly. "Everything's fine. I'll take care of it."

"I'm sensing you don't want me to come there."

"You're being paranoid." No, Jamie wasn't being paranoid, but no point in getting her all upset. The woman could be dangerous on her best days; no use risking an entire town when Emma could take care of the situation herself.

"I've got it all under control."

"Even though you're being held against your will by evil government forces busy creating giant, friendly Southern guys?"

"I'm hanging up now."

"Okay. Okay." Jamie laughed. "Before you go, the others will want to see you. Tonight."

"Why?"

"To make sure you're okay. And stop sounding so surprised. It's giving me a complex. Your place later. Okay?"

Finally, Emma laughed. "Yeah. My place."

"Good. Talk to you later."

"Okay." Emma grabbed hold of the doorknob, blinking when she noticed it was engraved with the hospital logo. That seemed a pricey expense for a local hospital. "Later, Jamie." She closed the phone and opened the door, coming face-to-face with an abnormally large chest. The phone snatched from her hand, Emma made a weird little squeak before raising her eyes up a delectable body to look into the deputy's handsome face.

"Theft," he said calmly, "is a hangin' offense in Smithville, sweetheart."

And Emma knew he was dead serious.

"You can't do this to me!"

He didn't even look up from the circle-track-racing magazine he had in his hands. "Yes. I can."

Emma stared down at the handcuff securing her right wrist to the metal frame of the bed. Still not quite believing what was happening, she clanged the metal cuff against the metal frame, which extracted a healthy growl from the deputy.

"Stop doing that. It's annoying me."

Too angry to be wary, Emma slammed the cuff against the metal again.

His head snapped up and those light gold eyes locked onto her.

Eep!

"I said, don't do that."

"And I said, let me go."

With a smirk, the bastard went back to his magazine. So Emma jangled the cuff.

His growl turned into a snarl. "You do know I can make this much worse for you?"

"And you do know I can sue you, this hospital, this weird little town, and anybody else I can think of? Do you know that?" She didn't know where these balls she suddenly had came from, but she had to admit she enjoyed them.

"And I can charge you with theft. Maybe you're hoping to see the inside of our jails."

"You'd put me in jail?" She couldn't keep the shock out of her voice. She was Emma Lucchesi. Boring Emma Lucchesi. Except for her tendency to speed on the Long Island Expressway, Emma never had any legal problems. She sure as hell never went to jail!

"It's crossed my mind." He leaned back in his chair. "Or you can tell me why you're here and we can forget all about your thieving ways."

"First off, I *borrowed* that phone. And second, I'm on vacation. Besides, I wouldn't have stopped in this town if I hadn't gotten lost and crashed my car."

"Which reminds me … How did that happen? The crash, I mean."

"Dog."

"Dog?"

"A dog ran out in the middle of the road. I swerved to avoid it."

"You sure it was a dog?"

"Yes. I'm sure it was a dog." From the seventh or eighth level of hell, but a dog.

He didn't argue with her, which made her more nervous than if he had.

His head tilted to the side as he studied her. "Why do you wear your hair in your face like that?"

Shocked again, Emma reared back a bit. "I'm sorry?"

"Why do you wear your hair like that? Can you even see?"

"Of course I can see!"

"Really? 'Cause you remind me of one of those sheepdogs, but I heard they can't see unless someone grooms their hair."

She took a deep breath and said, "Can we stop talking to each other now?"

"Why? I was enjoying our conversation." And she had the feeling he meant that.

"Well, I'm not. In fact, you're starting to annoy me. And I don't usually say that to people, even when they are. But you? You need to hear it."

"Fair enough." He went back to his magazine and didn't say another word.

Emma picked up one of the magazines he'd bought for her. She rolled her eyes at the fashion model on the cover.

"Not your thing?" And she realized even when she thought the man didn't pay any attention to her, he did.

She shook her head, tossing the magazine aside and searching through the rest of the pile. "Nope." She grabbed U.S. *News & World Report* and rested back against the pillows.

"Hmm. A thinker," he muttered and Emma almost laughed. But then she nearly choked when he added, "I like thinkers."

FOUR

Kyle heard her sigh in her sleep one too many times. He could not stand it. Pushing himself out of the chair, he left Emma's room. If he wanted to get any sleep tonight, he'd have to find another place to snooze, because every time the damn woman sighed, he got harder and harder until he was pretty sure he might explode.

He couldn't go far, not with her being pretty tricky. He still hadn't figured out how she got his phone off his jeans without him knowing. If she got out, he might have a hell of a time tracking her. And then he'd have to fight off every damn predator in town to protect her. One whiff of her delicious scent and they'd be all over her, too. He simply wouldn't tolerate it. Which was one of the reasons he'd handcuffed her to the bed. Well, that and she looked damn tasty wearing his handcuffs.

Stepping outside, Kyle breathed in the fresh air and felt the knots in his shoulders start to unwind a bit. He couldn't help but smile. He sure did love this town. Always had. Tourists came and went. Always in their fancy cars, with their annoying Yankee accents, and they brought in good money. But nothing about their lives outside of Smithville ever interested Kyle. Not when everything he wanted or needed was right here.

Even as he had that thought, a deer came running by, followed closely by the Smith Pack, Tully leading them.

As soon as he caught his brother's scent, Tully stopped, letting the Pack go on without him. He trotted up to Kyle, his one stupid hoop earring hanging from the tip of his dog ear. He was one of the few shifters Kyle knew who insisted on wearing identifying jewelry while animal. Their baby sister called him Pirate Dog.

Tully dropped his front down while his ass swung in the air. Kyle shook his head, but he couldn't fight the smile. "I can't. Forget it."

Charging forward a bit, Tully nipped at his jeans and jumped back.

Well, a man did have to eat.

"All right. Fine." Kyle pulled off his T-shirt. "But we can't go too far from the hospital. I gotta keep my eye on Little Miss Trouble in there."

Kyle shucked his clothes, tossing them in a safe bin beside the front door. The hospital staff used it when they needed to go for a run or get in some hunting. Shifting, the black cat took off after his brother, tackling him and tossing him ten feet before tearing after the hot meal running away from them.

Emma slept. She knew she did because she was awake in her dreamscape. As a controller of her own dreams, she'd built her dreamscape from the bottom up, and she absolutely loved it. A perfect aqua blue ocean, blue sand, a low-hanging and giant light burgundy moon, and palm trees. She didn't come here every night, but when stressed, she headed to the one place where she felt calm.

Of course her Coven sisters weren't letting her rest yet. They wanted to see her, to make sure she was really okay. So they kept calling to her, like someone leaning on her doorbell. Grudgingly, she used her power to yank her Coven from their realm into hers.

"Emma!" Seneca Kuroki threw her arms around Emma and hugged her tight. "Oh, God! I'm so glad you are okay. I was so worried."

Emma gave Sen another two seconds before she gently but firmly pulled the woman's arms off her. "I'm fine, Sen. Really."

"Wow, Em. You really did a lot with this place," Kendall Cohen remarked softly, looking around Emma's dreamscape.

"Thanks."

"I see the Master of Dreams title was fairly earned." Jamie grinned at her. "You look okay."

"I'm fine. That hillbilly Nazi took the phone from me."

"Probably because you stole it."

"I borrowed it. But do you think he listens? No. He just handcuffs me to the bed like a common criminal."

As one, her Coven turned to face her, clearly no longer interested in the surrounding beauty of the place she'd created.

She stared back. "What?"

Jamie tilted her head to the side, and Emma could see her desperately trying not to laugh. "He handcuffed you to the bed?"

"Yeah. So?"

Kenny placed her hands on her hips. "Isn't that a tad kinky, Em? You know … for you."

Wearing a T-shirt that read "I *am* Lord of the Rings," Kenny remained the biggest geek Emma knew. At thirty-two, Kenny seemed to be comfortably staying in her tomboy phase, not only with her short, shaggy haircut and geek T-shirt, but also those very worn jeans, bright red high-top

Keds she'd drawn dragons all over, and a leather armband
Ken once drunkenly admitted made her feel like "a total
warrior chick." Kenny even turned her one wasted year at
MIT—with that whopping 1.7 GPA—into a gaming career
that made her more money than seemed humanly possible. It still boggled Emma that there were game packages
in Europe and Asia with Kenny's name on the cover. And
Emma would bet cash that Kenny had fallen asleep on her
couch with her four-thousand-dollar computer in her lap.
Of the five of them, Kenny was the only one fully dressed
rather than in nightclothes.

"If it were you, Kendall, maybe. But this is me we're talking about. Me and kinky... not close friends."

They all watched Seneca, the pretty waitress from
Manhasset and the necessary balance of good for their
dark little Coven, spin around them. Literally. "I feel so free
here!" More than thirteen years since Sen led their old high
school in a cheer, and still the woman acted like pom-poms
were permanently attached to her.

Kenny crossed her eyes and sighed. If they weren't in
the same coven, Kenny probably would have beaten Seneca
to death a long time ago. Sen's bone-deep perkiness wore
on Kenny's nerves something awful. Emma didn't mind
Sen, though. She was just so damn cute, it was hard not to
like her.

"Come on, Em. Give it up. You and the deputy doing
something morally reprehensible with those cuffs?"
Mackenzie Mathews, dressed in loose sweatpants and a
tank top, stood next to her cousin. Actually, she stood over
her. Except for the fact both women were black and related
by their mothers, there was very little else in common
between them. Mac, a good six-foot-three in her bare feet,
always kept her head. She rarely panicked, never became

hysterical, and kept her cousin in check. Her straight black hair barely reached her shoulders and the blue tank top she wore showed the very large and powerful muscles she got from her hard work. Jamie, on the other hand, stood a good five inches shorter than her cousin, her long hair curly and usually in a ponytail for work. A lighter brown than Mac and a hell of a lot curvier, Jamie remained their "loose cannon." The woman had immense power and knew how to use it. But it was her Coven that kept her from doing something incredibly stupid. It was her Coven that kept her from becoming evil and trying to take over the world.

"As you see"—Emma wanted her privacy, so time to hurry this along—"I'm fine."

When no one said anything, Emma's eyes narrowed. "What?"

"You really think we did this?" Jamie asked.

"Do I think we opened the doorway? Yeah. Do I think we unleashed that thing … that I don't know. But if I were a gambler I'd probably put money on it."

"Jamie thinks someone wanted us down here." Mac adjusted her wide stance and rubbed her left lower back. The wound she had there still hurt even after five months, although they were starting to think it was more in her mind than a true physical pain. Not surprising. After what happened. After the attack.

"Has anyone approached you? Or said anything?" Jamie walked over to her cousin and placed her palm flat against the spot where a blade had been brutally shoved between two ribs. Her hand glowed for a moment, then she said softly, "There. That should help the pain." It wasn't until that horrible night at the hospital, waiting on Mac's doctors to come out of surgery, that the Coven realized how much Mac meant to Jamie. No matter how much Jamie might deny it.

"No." Emma answered Jamie's original question. "I've only dealt with that idiot cop and the hospital staff. But they do seem real curious why I'm here. Like they're not big on strangers."

"Wait," Kenny interrupted. "Are you trying to say they don't 'cotton to outsiders 'round here'?"

Emma laughed. "Yeah. That's about the size of it."

"Well, you're a better woman than I, Em." Kenny watched Seneca spin by her again. "I would be freaking out right about now with my ass trapped in North Carolina." Ken stuck her foot out and Seneca gracefully leaped right over it, turned, and gave Kenny the finger. Then the little brat did the Cabbage Patch at her.

Emma rubbed her eyes. "Why would anyone mess with us?" True, to the rest of the world, Emma was invisible. She didn't exist. She, like her reliable Toyota, was beige. But her Coven...well, that was a different story. Most witches stayed out of their way. Good or evil, they all gave the Coven of the Darkest Night a wide berth. In their minds the fact that Emma's coven didn't firmly play for one side or the other bothered most covens. Especially after that one incident that got them banned for life from the Green Man Festival.

But for Emma and her sisters it wasn't a simple case of black or white, good or evil. Because sometimes, when things went bad, you did what you had to do. Emma's Coven wasn't afraid to fight mean. Hell, they were good at it.

So exactly what idiot would be fool enough to lure them to this boring town in the middle of nowhere, North Carolina? And...why the hell had she been stupid enough to agree to come?

Kyle slammed his paw against Tully's muzzle, ripping his claws through the fur. Tully flipped back, but came at him again. Kyle didn't wait. He went to the tallest tree and climbed it, dragging his prize with him. Once he found a comfortable limb, he lay down to eat. The wolves circled under the tree, watching him, waiting for him to drop some morsel and planning. As always, the hunt went from simple fun to deadly dangerous once they had their prey in their sights. Out-of-town shifters learned fast that Smithville wasn't a leisurely town when it came to the hunting. It often turned mean and vicious with so many different breeds fighting over the prey. But for Kyle, that's what he loved.

Enjoying his warm meal—especially once it stopped squirming—Kyle chewed and stared, keeping a lookout for any other hungry predators. Once, one of the tourist-tigers had leaped up and snagged Kyle's meal right from him before landing back on the ground like nothing had happened. And more than one lion had climbed up after him. He'd given his prize up since the fuckers were so big, but they could never get down from those trees again, which Kyle found immensely entertaining.

Soon another prey charged by and Tully's Pack went after it, leaving Kyle to his hot meal. He ate until he was full and then he leaped down from the tree, leaving his prize behind. He didn't finish it so, in theory, he could share...but he didn't share. Wolves shared. Lions shared when there was enough to go around. He, however, did not share unless he was human—and his momma slapped him in the back of the head telling him to act right.

Kyle sauntered back to the hospital, only a mile or so away, and found another tree right outside the Yankee's room. Taking a limb not too far from the ground, he got comfortable and watched the woman. He could see her lying in her bed, asleep, handcuffed to the railing. The thought had him purring, moments before he dropped off to sleep.

Lying against her blue sand, Emma stared up at the sky she'd created. A little too bright. She took it down a notch until the sky became more a pale navy than a bright cerulean.

Emma had two days. Two days to destroy whatever had tried to kill her and to get home. After that, her Coven would be coming for her, and she'd prefer to avoid that. The five of them together could cause all sorts of problems. From the time they'd all met in ninth-grade Social Studies, they'd been a functioning unit. A business partnership, almost. Each serving a purpose, each fulfilling a specific role. Emma always knew, though, if it weren't for the Coven they probably wouldn't be friends. They were too different and had very little in common except the witchcraft.

Jamie always said they were more family than friends. Friends you chose, while family was forced upon you. Still, Emma liked them all and tolerated them fairly well. And she liked that no matter what, they watched out for each other. They definitely treated Emma better than her own siblings did. It didn't even occur to Emma to call her own blood relatives after the accident. They always thought her weird and said it often, especially when the wine began to flow at family dinners. Her parents tried to make it easier on her, but they all knew she didn't belong. Kind of like the runt of the litter.

Emma shook her head, not wanting to think about it anymore. She came to her dreamscape to relax and just be, and that's what she planned to do.

A rabbit darted past her and Emma watched it with a smile. She did love rabbits. They were the only pets she ever had. Dogs were way too messy and cats simply freaked her out. They always stared at her like they knew she'd been up to something. Considering she was usually up to very little, that reaction seemed strange. Rabbits, however, were cute and fluffy and didn't have claws. You just had to watch out for their sharp teeth, and their feet could kick you pretty good. It was their only defense, though, against animals higher on the food chain.

Like the giant black cat racing past her.

Emma blinked and sat up straight. Why in hell was there a panther in her dreamscape? She never had cats in her dreamscape. Not that she could stop them if they wanted in. Animals could come and go as they pleased through anyone's dreams, but she'd never had some big jungle cat come charging into her sacred space.

Even more disturbing, the cat caught the rabbit, shook it, tossed it in the air, caught it, and started shaking it again. Emma squealed, horrified, and the cat spun around, the poor rabbit still in its mouth. It stared at Emma and she stared back. From muzzle to ass it had to be well over six feet and easily weighed two hundred plus pounds. Its tail alone looked to be about four to five feet. Still, like most things in the universe, it didn't even notice her until she made that stupid noise.

She wasn't going to run. This was her dreamscape, goddammit! She created it. She controlled it.

The panther spat out the rabbit, and the bunny took off. Then the big cat walked toward her, its big paws slapping against the sand as it moved closer and closer. Emma still held her ground, refusing to run. But every chant she tried simply didn't work. She used all her tricks to push the fucking thing out of her dreamscape and out of her head, but nothing worked.

Finally, it stood in front of her. Cold light gold eyes stared at her, watching her with an intense curiosity that was making her extremely uncomfortable.

Emma glared at it. "Go away," she ordered it. "You're not welcome here."

It made a rather rude snorting noise like it didn't believe that for one second. Then it stepped closer to her, its smooth black fur brushing against her skin as it rubbed up against her, its large head pushing into her as it moved around her body. It purred and nuzzled the back of her neck, its breath warm and sweet against her flesh.

Emma felt naked. Since it was her dreamscape, she'd changed into a dark red bikini after her Coven left. A bikini she'd never have the guts to wear in the real world. Now she tried to conjure a parka and full body armor, anything to protect her soft, exposed flesh from those *really* giant claws. But she couldn't focus. Not when she couldn't look away from the beast moving toward her.

The cat brushed against her leg and then side, moving around her and rubbing itself up against her body. She swallowed back a lump of panic as its tail dragged along her thighs and up across her chest, settling around her neck. The tip brushed the flesh right below her ear. And, surprisingly, that felt kind of nice.

Settling down behind her, its body snuggled up against hers, the cat rested its head comfortably on her thigh. Then he purred.

Oh! And wasn't *that* an interesting feeling.

Trying to control her breathing, Emma glanced down at the big cat. "Comfortable?"

In answer, the cat rubbed its head against her thigh, and then licked the back of the opposite knee.

"Okay, feel free to stop doing that."

In response, it slid its head up her thigh, and Emma put her hand on his snout to halt its progress. "Don't even think about putting your nose there. A girl's gotta have some dignity."

A grumble came up from the cat's chest, and she wondered if that was its laugh.

The fact it didn't try to take her arm off had her smiling a bit, so Emma gently ran her fingers across its head. When it merely snuggled in closer, she dug deep into its coat. Its muscles rippled under her fingers and the purring became decidedly louder. She tickled the backs of its ears and massaged its big neck.

"You are the cutest thing, aren't you?"

All seemed to be going well … until it started moving up her body. Emma's hand froze as the big cat dragged its head across her stomach and chest while the rest of it unwound from behind her and slowly moved over her.

Emma slapped her hands against its shoulders, trying to push it off. Unfortunately, the big bastard wouldn't budge, and panic had settled in quite nicely.

She really had no idea how to handle this. Except for what she'd learned from occasionally being too lazy to change the channel when a documentary on jungle animals came on TV, Emma knew next to nothing about the animal kingdom and what to do when a big cat decided to use your body as a scratching post.

The cat loomed over her now, staring down at her. Nope. She didn't like the look in those eyes one damn bit.

Clearly it was time for one of her full-blown panic attacks. She hadn't had one of those since Jamie "accidentally" took the Coven to hell in the eleventh grade—something they still hadn't completely forgiven their high priestess for.

Before she could lose all rational thought and start screaming, those scary cat muscles under her fingers rippled and the fur ... retreated, sliding back inside the cat's body. Then the cat face hovering over her began to shift and change, as did the cat body sliding between her legs.

Then he was there. The good-old-boy deputy now stared down at her, his naked body fitting comfortably between her legs. The only thing that didn't change ... those eyes.

He gave her that slow, easy grin of his and said, "Hello, darlin'."

"Uh ... Deputy."

"If I'm gonna dream about you, the least you can do is call me Kyle."

"Kyle." How pathetic. Now she was conjuring up strange hillbillies in her dreamscape. Had it really been *that* long since she'd last gotten laid? Was she truly this pathetic?

He glanced down at her body. "I *like* this bikini, Emma." And it sounded like he sort of growled that compliment. "You look really good in it."

She rolled her eyes. Yup, she'd become *that* pathetic.

What else would her dream Kyle say? Maybe he'd tell her she was hot and he wanted to fuck her all night long. Ooh. Or maybe he'd say, "I've been waiting my entire life for you, Emma Lucchesi."

Pathetic. Pathetic. Pathetic.

Putting all his weight on one arm, Kyle brought his other hand up and brushed his big fingers across the exposed skin of her shoulder and down her arm.

"So soft," he murmured.

She snorted a laugh and he looked at her, still smiling. "What's so funny, darlin'?"

"Me. My dreams. I mean, since I'm going hog wild, I should have conjured up Ares or Thor. Or had all three of you!" She nodded her head. "Now that is dreaming, my friend."

"You think you can handle all three of us?" he teased.

"Hey. It's my dreamscape. I'm a frickin' goddess of love here."

"I had no idea Yankees could be so funny. Especially you New York types."

"It's how we survive the rough-and-tumble streets of Long Island."

Okay. She'd admit it. This was strange and fun. She couldn't remember the last time she'd dreamed about another human being. But it *had* been ages since she'd been with a man, and to be quite honest, she was a little horny. Had been since she saw the deputy standing over her at the beach.

Hell, what was she fighting here? It was merely a stupid wet dream. She might as well enjoy it before she woke up in her continually empty bed.

Slipping her arms around his neck, Emma smiled up into his surprised face.

She sighed. "I have to say, you are really hot, Deputy."

"Why thank you, ma'am."

"You're welcome." She cleared her throat and said, "Kiss me, Kyle."

He grinned, slow and lazy, his head dipping down and his lips hovering right over hers. "Where I come from, we always try and do what the lady asks."

Emma's eyes closed as his breath brushed her lips. "Good to know."

He didn't dive right for her lips like she thought he would. Instead, he brushed his forehead against hers, nuzzled her chin with his nose, and rubbed his cheek along her jaw. He moved slow and easy, like he had all the time in the world.

It dawned on Emma she had no control over Dream-Kyle, which seemed strange. She had control over everything else in her dreamscape but the animals. Maybe the fact she'd first envisioned him as a panther caused this, but she couldn't seem to rush him. Couldn't seem to force him to do anything she wanted.

When his lips finally touched hers, it was nothing more than a gentle caress. Their breath barely mingled.

Her body moved under his, trying to get closer, and wetness began to seep from between her legs. Frustrated, she tightened her arms around his neck and tried to pull him closer, but he only smiled.

"Easy, darlin'. There ain't no rush."

"I'm from New York. We move much faster there."

"That's a real shame," he murmured as he lowered their bodies to stretch out on the sand. "Y'all don't know what you've been missing."

Before she could respond, he kissed her. No mere touching of lips, this. No, there was real intent and hunger behind this kiss, and Emma immediately opened her mouth to him. His tongue touched hers and she groaned, desperate for more. Desperate for him. As his tongue explored her mouth, he pried her arms off his neck, gripping both her wrists in one big hand while pinning her arms over her head.

In real life she'd be terrified if some guy she barely knew held her down like this but, as Kenny would say, "Fuck it." It was her dreamscape, and if Dream-Kyle wanted to be all alpha dog on her, who was she to argue?

Besides ... she liked it.

Kyle's free hand slid down her neck, her shoulder, and settled on her breast. He squeezed and Emma arched into his hand, a soft moan torn from her throat. Strong fingers toyed with her nipple until it stood hard and ripe. That's when Kyle stopped kissing her. Panting, she stared up at him.

Kyle squeezed her nipple again between his thumb and forefinger. Emma gasped, desperately fighting to pull her hands out of his grasp, if for no other reason than to get herself off.

Kyle lowered his head, and she watched his lips wrap around her bikini-covered breast. He sucked hard and Emma felt herself unraveling. She slammed her thighs together, trying to create some friction, trying to throw herself over the edge. But then Kyle's free hand was there, forcing its way between her legs and under her bikini bottom. He slid two big fingers inside her pussy, and his thumb played mercilessly with her clit.

The rush of power slammed through her and Emma turned her head, burying her face in her upper arm. Emma bit hard into her own flesh to stifle her cry as the orgasm roared through her. So intense, she tried to pull away, but Kyle wouldn't release her. His hand tightened on her wrists, his mouth on her breast, and his fingers found a spot inside her that he caressed over and over again.

She didn't know if she came again or if it just kept on rolling. All Emma knew was that she'd never felt anything like it before.

In dreams or out.

Finally, the strength of her orgasm forced her teeth to tear past skin, the pain shoving her right out of her dreams and right back into her hospital room.

Jerking awake, Emma looked into strange hazel eyes.

"Who...who the hell are you?" she panted out.

"And a good morning to you, too, sunshine. Hope I didn't scare you." A slow, easy grin spread across a handsome face. "I'm Tully Smith, Kyle's bigger and much better-looking brother."

FIVE

Kyle snapped awake and, for the first time in his entire life, he lost his grip on the limb his body lay across—and fell out of the tree, hitting the ground hard, panting and goddamn horny. His eyes flickered around as he desperately tried to get his bearings.

He looked up into the faces of two nurses he and Tully once had quite a good time with at one of the town's annual barbecues.

"Hi, Kyle," one said, laughing as they walked around him, "Good thing it's warm out this mornin', huh, darlin'?"

That's when Kyle realized he'd shifted back to human sometime during the night. He'd never done that before. However he went to sleep was how he woke up.

It must have been because of that damn dream that seemed so real he imagined he could still feel the sticky wetness of Emma's pussy on his fingers.

How he'd gone from chasing rabbits to making one hot, adorable Emma Lucchesi come, he had no idea. He didn't appreciate the damn dream ending, either, before he had the chance to bury himself inside the woman.

That bikini. That bikini had been his undoing. Once he saw her in that damn red bikini, he couldn't keep his paws off her. Hell, what red-blooded American male could?

Plus, for once, she didn't look panicked or scared or shy. Instead, she seemed damn relaxed and comfortable. She even hit on him. That's when he knew it was only a dream. But why should he fight a good wet dream?

Lord in Heaven, he thought those sounds she made while sleeping were sexy. Those didn't hold a candle to the sounds she made while coming.

Never before had Kyle regretted a dream ending as much as he did this one. Especially when he felt like he could still taste Emma's skin on his tongue.

Nothing had ever tasted sweeter.

Blinking hard to snap himself out of it, Kyle sat up. He needed to distract himself before he did something stupid. Like storm into Emma's room and take her right there in her hospital bed.

No, no. Bad idea. He'd have a hot breakfast first, like the elk he could smell somewhere nearby, and then he'd be right as rain and would be able to face one Emma Lucchesi—hopefully not wearing that damn bikini.

He'd never survive her in that bikini.

"We're not blood. Me and Kyle. His daddy took it upon himself to defile my momma. To ruin her pure innocence."

Laughing, Emma asked, "Um ... she already had you. So how innocent could she—"

"She was innocent and I won't hear any different. This is nothing more than an unholy alliance as far as I'm concerned."

For some unfathomable reason, Emma liked Kyle's brother. She definitely liked him way more than she liked Kyle. Tully could talk to anyone, it seemed. Emma always had a hard time holding conversations. Small talk had never been her friend, but Tully Smith made it easy even while she knew his presence here wasn't merely altruistic.

Besides, around Tully she didn't get all ... squirmy.

"Don't you have a baby sister, though, because of this unholy alliance?"

"The only good thing to come out of it, if you ask me."

"What about your real father?"

"Ah, yes. My real father. Well, Miss Emma, he's what they would have called in ancient times a bastard. And we avoid each other's company as much as possible."

Tully looked at her hospital door. "You gonna stand out there all day, hoss, or are you coming in?"

Emma frowned and glanced at the door. "Who are you talking—"

The door opened and the biggest man Emma had ever seen in her entire existence walked in carrying the duffel bag she'd brought with her from New York.

So tall, the man's head nearly touched the ceiling; so wide she wondered how he got through the damn door. Well into the three-hundred-pound range but without an ounce of fat on him, his body wasn't awkward because of its size. Instead, it was perfectly proportioned.

Like Kyle, this man wore black boots, black jeans, and a black T-shirt with the Smithville County Sheriff's Department logo stitched in white on the front. But he also had on a black baseball cap with the same logo.

Brown hair, brown eyes, and, except for that rather permanent-looking frown on his face, incredibly handsome.

"Miss Emma, this is Sheriff Bear McMahon. And yes, Bear's his real name. Bear, this is Emma Lucchesi, our little accidental visitor."

The sheriff touched the rim of his hat. "Ma'am."

Holy shit. Emma had never heard a voice that low before.

Say something, you idiot. Don't just stare at the man. "Nice to meet you, Sheriff."

"I'm glad you're here, Bear." Tully stood up. "I want to take our Miss Emma to breakfast in the cafeteria, but your deputy has made that impossible."

"What?"

Tully took Emma's hand and lifted it so Bear could see the handcuff.

"And," she added, a bit desperately, "to be quite honest, I really have to go."

Dropping her duffel bag on an empty chair, Bear sighed and walked over to Emma.

"Some days I wonder 'bout that boy."

"I know," Tully agreed with a small smile that didn't seem at all brotherly. "I don't know how you trust him with human lives."

As Bear leaned over to let her loose, Tully gave her a slow wink and she nearly shivered. Dangerous. This man was very nice and very dangerous.

"There." Bear removed the cuffs and slipped them into the back pocket of his jeans.

Emma scooted off the bed and grabbed her duffel bag. "Thanks."

"We'll wait outside until you're done," Bear offered.

Tully snorted. "We will?"

With a low grunt, Bear grabbed Tully by the back of the neck and shoved him out the door.

Emma nearly sprinted to the bathroom and gratefully used the toilet, trying hard to keep her relieved sighs to herself. Once done, she dropped the bag on top of the closed toilet and reached back to untie the gown. That's when she felt it. A deep, painful sting. Panic swept through her, and she practically tore the gown from her body. She stood in front of the mirror over the sink and raised her left arm.

Then she stared.

She stared at the clear bite mark on the inside of her upper arm. Right where she'd put it when Dream-Kyle made her come. Of course, with her arm handcuffed to the bed, that was physically impossible to do in her sleep unless...

Well, this just got horribly weird.

Kyle walked into Emma's hospital room freshly showered, dressed and fed, only to find the woman and his favorite pair of handcuffs gone.

Finding her gone only irritated him a little. The lingering scent of his mongrel brother and that flea-bitten bear, though, had him spitting mad.

"Bastards."

Focusing on Emma's scent rather than Tully's or Bear's, Kyle found them easily enough. They sat at a long table in the cafeteria eating a typically large Smithville breakfast.

Kyle hung back by the entryway and watched Emma, all that hair still partially covering her face. Like a sucker punch to his gut, all those intense feelings from the dream came rushing back to him, holding his body and his mind hostage.

Damn the woman. Damn her to hell and back.

Without a word, Kyle stormed over to the table and sat in the chair opposite Tully and catty-corner from Emma. Bear, by his very nature and size, always needed more space, so he sat three chairs over.

"I turn my back for ten seconds," Kyle stated while grabbing a link sausage off Emma's plate, "and you disappear on me."

Emma picked up a slice of toast and bit into it, all while staring at him, but she didn't say a word.

"Lord, little brother, you sure are cranky this lovely summer morning."

Without taking his eyes off Emma, Kyle said, "Shut up, Tully."

"I wonder what has you so tense. Could it be the daily stresses of your job? Are your Wranglers too tight? Has that stick up your ass gotten bigger?"

Emma laughed, and Kyle turned on Tully like a rattler on a mongoose.

"Go chase your tail, mongrel."

"Go climb a tree."

"Go chew a toy."

"Go play with yarn."

They were ten seconds away from going after each other with fangs and claws whether completely human Emma was there or not, but the growled "Y'all" immediately calmed them down. Only Bear had that ability. The man could make "y'all" sound like the scariest thing ever.

Kyle glanced at his boss. "Hey, Bear."

"Kyle."

And that's all Bear said. A man of few words, Sheriff McMahon kept the town safe and everyone in line simply by being what he was...a big bear. They were the perfect breed for sheriff. No affiliations except with their own kin. No Packs, Prides or Clans to speak of. They didn't like anyone, really, even each other, so favoritism was never a big problem. And whether human or bear, they were enormous, so even tigers at sometimes seven hundred pounds when shifted had to think twice before challenging them. Bear's ability to defuse brawls between lions and hyenas had become legendary.

As long as you stayed out of their way and didn't make too much noise when they were around, brown and black bears made great law enforcers.

Bear took his position from Momma McMahon, and one day Bear's fifteen-year-old son, Luke, would probably do the same. If for no other reason, the McMahons really didn't feel like going anywhere else and starting over. Bears liked their lives simple and quiet. And Kyle's boss was no different.

Sopping gravy with his biscuit, Bear asked, "Can you explain to me, Deputy, why Miss Emma was wearing your handcuffs this morning?"

"She stole my phone."

"Borrowed," she squeaked in. "I *borrowed* your phone."

Bear silently chewed his biscuit for several long seconds, then said to Emma, "You do know stealing is a hanging offense around here, don't ya?"

Emma threw up her hands. "It is not! And stop saying that. You're freaking me out."

Going back to his biscuits and gravy, Bear grumbled, "I'm just saying'…it could have been worse for ya."

Even though she rolled her eyes in exasperation, Emma still smiled. A smile that had Kyle staring at her like a love-sick cub. He didn't even realize it until Tully kicked him under the table to snap him out of it.

Completely oblivious, Emma sipped her orange juice and said to Tully, "Finish your story."

"Oh, yeah. Anyway, I was a tender fifteen. She a saucy eighteen-year-old—"

"Not that," Emma laughed. "I meant about your family."

"Oh. Well. You've got your Carolina Smiths. North and South. Your Alabama Smiths. Your Tennessee Smiths. Your Kentucky Smiths. And your Texas Smiths, but they ain't real friendly. As well as Florida, Detroit, and, of course, the West Virginia Smiths."

Kyle glanced at Emma and shrugged. "Of course."

Emma giggled as Tully continued.

"But it all started right here when the first Smith arrived on these shores about four hundred years ago."

"You can trace your family back that far?"

"Most of us around here can."

Emma shrugged. "I know I have a great-aunt on my dad's side who lives in Sicily, and a cousin on my mom's side in Jiaoling Prison for gunrunning."

Kyle sighed. "Well, isn't that a lovely tale to tell your grandchildren one day."

Emma held her arm up so Kyle could see her wrist. "Did you notice this? I'm bruised from your stupid handcuffs."

"Then you shouldn't steal," he said while stealing another sausage link off her plate. "So ... did you sleep well, Emma?"

Emma choked on her juice, waving Kyle away when he went to pound on her back.

She'd been trying all morning to forget about that dream and praying he didn't remember. The more she thought about it, the more she realized she must have pulled the poor sap right into her dreamscape. Based on the way he was looking at her, though, he hadn't forgotten a damn thing.

Wiping her mouth with a linen napkin embroidered with the hospital's logo, Emma muttered, "I slept well. The beds here are very soft and comfortable. For a hospital and all."

"We do like our creature comforts," Tully offered after sipping his coffee. "When you check out of the hospital, you can stay at the Smithville Arms and—" Tully abruptly stopped speaking, those dangerous hazel eyes locking on Kyle. "Do that again and you'll lose a leg, son."

That's when Emma knew Kyle had kicked his brother under the table.

"Mind your own business or I'll rip out your throat."

Emma had seen a lot of fights between men. Before college, she worked in her father's Manhasset pizza parlor every summer. After eight o'clock on a Saturday night, after a few pitchers of beer, there was always a fight between two or more guys. Lots of bullshit threats thrown around. Occasionally the cops called. But something about these two squaring off felt different.

It felt... deadly.

"Y'all," Bear sighed again, either not feeling the tension or not caring. And like that, the deadly moment ended as quickly as it had come.

Bear finished off his juice and stood up, pulling his baseball cap out of his back pocket. "I'm done eating. I'm going back to the office. Nice to meet you, Miss Emma. See ya at the office, Kyle. You coming, Tully?"

"Nope. I think I'm going to spend a little more time with our Miss Emma."

Our?

Kyle hadn't felt this pissed since a bunch of hyenas surrounded him and took off with his deer. He'd hunted it, run it down, torn it open, and then these scavengers came out of nowhere and his one to their twenty didn't stand a chance. He had to let his prize go:

He'd be damned if he did the same thing with Emma. He especially wouldn't give her up to Tully. The woman deserved better than a dog.

Emma leaned forward, dropping her head in her hands, her. fingers rubbing her eyes in obvious exasperation. "Look, Deputy, I'm really fine and I think—"

"Why do you always have your hair in your face like that?"

Her hands froze and, after several seconds, brown eyes stared at him through her fingers and all that hair. "What is your obsession with my hair?"

He ignored her question to ask his own. "You do know you're pretty, don't you? You're not insecure about that, are you?"

Emma glared at him. "I don't think you said that loud enough. Utah missed out."

"If you don't believe me, ask Tully. He'll be honest."

A look of horror spread across her face and a strangled sound came out of her throat. "No!"

Tully grinned. "Ask me."

Kyle turned to his brother. "Do you think Emma's—" He stopped speaking. He had to. The large piece of ham that hit him in the head completely distracted him.

Tully snorted out a laugh and looked away.

Kyle squinted at Emma. "Did you just hit me with pork?"

"I had to."

"You *had* to?"

"Yes. You wouldn't shut up," she squeaked.

Tully laughed harder and Kyle joined him, tossing the ham onto the table. It had been a long time since they found something to laugh at together. Most of the time it was more about keeping territory, fighting over prey, or getting the bigger piece of their momma's pecan pie at Thanksgiving dinner.

"It's not funny," she yelped.

"Actually..." The brothers looked at each other and said in unison, "Yes, it is!"

Growling, Emma poked at what was left of her food. "Let's just leave Tully out of this."

"Why? What are you afraid he's going to say?"

"It's not what he'll say. It's what he won't say. It's The Pause."

Kyle and Tully glanced at each other. "The Pause?" Kyle asked, finding himself damn entertained by this woman.

"Yeah. The Pause."

"And what is that exactly?"

Emma tucked her legs up under her and sat back on her heels. "It's when someone asks you a question that you start to answer honestly and realize you can't, you stand there staring blindly for two seconds too long and your true answer becomes clear."

When neither brother said anything, she elaborated. "For instance, 'Honey? Do I look fat in this?' And your only response is to stare for more than fifteen seconds because you're scrambling for an answer. Like this..." Her face went perfectly blank under all that hair. Then she shrugged. "That's The Pause."

It was the most the woman had said at one time, and he found it...wonderful. She wore her nuttiness well.

"So, you were afraid Tully would give you The Pause if I asked him if you were cute?"

"It's possible. And I'm already too traumatized to have to stress over that as well."

"Sweetheart," Tully drawled, "you're not cute. You're hot. There's a difference. And I prefer hot any day."

Emma snorted. "Yeah. I'm sure that line gets you a lot of booty, Tully, but it won't work on me."

Tully leaned back in his chair and laughed. "Lord, woman. You are adorable." He looked at Kyle. "Let's keep her."

Kyle shrugged. "Okay."

"Wait. Wait. Wait." Emma shook her head. "I thought we discussed this. You can't just keep me."

"Why not?" Kyle and Tully asked together.

"'Cause I'm not a stray cat or something you found by the side of the road."

Tully grinned. "You mean like Kyle?" Tully leaned over and said, "His daddy don't like to talk about it, but he picked Kyle up over on Jessup Road hidin' under a car."

Kyle wanted to be mad, but he couldn't. Not with Emma around. "Yeah. And your momma told me she got you from the pound. Had you fixed there, too."

Emma scratched her forehead while pushing her food tray away. "You two slam each other with the weirdest insults."

Six

Emma, her hand on her hospital door, stopped and turned around to look at Tully. "I'm sorry. What?"

"I said I have to get back to my office."

"Before that."

"That being mayor is a lot of work."

She frowned. "Mayor of what?"

Kyle laughed so hard, she knew someone must have asked the question before.

With a small snarl, Tully answered, "Of Smithville."

"Oh, I see."

"Come on." Kyle shoved Tully hard, but the big man barely noticed. Boy, these Southerners were a tough bunch. "I need to talk to you outside for a sec, Mr. *Mayor*." As the pair headed down the hallway, Kyle threw over his shoulder, "And don't try sneaking off, darlin'. Unless you're just in the mood for me to hunt you down."

Emma didn't answer Kyle, too busy staring at his ass as he walked away. Jeez, the guy could really work a pair of jeans.

"Get control of yourself, you idiot." It was one thing to fool around with a guy in her dreamscape. A whole other thing to try it on this plane of existence. The risk of rejection was too great; she immediately dismissed the idea.

Emma didn't do embarrassment well. Actually, she didn't do it at all.

Sighing in resignation, she opened her hospital-room door and stopped.

"Uh…" She looked up at the number on the door to see if she had the wrong room. Nope. Right room.

The two very old women stared at her and she stared back.

"You must be Emma," one of them said.

"Yes. I am."

"I'm Sophie Winchell and this is my sister Adelaide." The second sister merely nodded in Emma's direction but apparently didn't feel the need to speak.

"Can I help you?"

"Oh, we're just here to visit. We heard you had a very bad accident."

"Around here that's big news." The other sister finally spoke, and Emma wished she hadn't. It sounded like someone shredded her vocal chords with a cheese grater.

"That's very nice of you."

"Not really," Adelaide admitted. "We just wanted to get a look atcha."

And that's when Emma knew. "Well, thanks for the welcome, sisters."

Sophie smiled but her sister sneered. "We ain't your sisters."

Emma sighed. "I see." All that light and love among certain covens, and still sometimes they could be the biggest bigots when it came to those who worshipped the Dark Mothers. "So then why am I here?"

The two sisters looked at each other and then Adelaide helped her sister out of the chair. Sophie used a cane, while her sister appeared to be as strong as an ox despite her obvious age. "You're here, dear, because we need you. Because we need your Coven."

The two women neared the door and Emma moved aside to let them pass. "They're not coming."

Sophie stopped and her sister began to say something, but Sophie cut her off with a raised hand. Adelaide might be the enforcer of their coven, but Sophie was definitely their high priestess.

"You should come stay at our hotel, the Smithville Arms, when you get out of here, dear. I think you'll like it. I think you'll definitely like this town. It's a good, safe place for our people."

Sophie raised her hand to pat Emma's cheek, but Emma stepped back and away.

The old woman smiled. "We'll talk when you feel better, dear." Without another word, the two women left.

"Looks like the big pussy's got a crush."

Kyle bared his fangs. "Stay away from her, Tully."

Tully gave a rough laugh. "I ain't a hyena, friend. I don't take what ain't mine."

"Who said she's mine?"

"You do. You're acting like you did last night when you dragged that gazelle up the tree so my Pack couldn't get to it. Besides"—Tully lifted his nose in the air and cast around—"something's not right in this town, little brother. You and I both know it. Soon everyone will know it. We can smell it on the wind. Feel it tremble beneath our feet in the dirt. There's something the Elders aren't telling us." Cold wolf eyes looked at Kyle, and he realized there was little connection between some fun-loving dog and the wolves that roamed Smithville. Although he did love watching Tully go all cranky when Kyle called him Fido.

Ambling off down the road, Tully said, "And what do you wanna bet, little brother, your Miss Emma is at the heart of it all?"

Emma stared out the window of her hospital room at the rapidly darkening sky. Seemed like it would be a stormy night.

The sky turned black quickly, nearly making Emma forget it wasn't even late afternoon yet. Trees swayed as the wind picked up, and she studied the forest behind the hospital.

Placing her hands against the glass, she leaned in closer and narrowed her eyes a bit, trying to see well into the trees. That's when she saw it. Two burning, bright red spots of light. Her nose touched the glass as she leaned in more. The light disappeared and quickly reappeared. *Blinking?*

Holy shit.

Emma stared hard into the growing darkness, her focus on those red spots and a powerful spell on her lips. But before she could unleash it—and possibly destroy the entire forest in the process—a strong arm reached around her, the fingers touching the glass.

"I guess you're going to see one of our storms, darlin'."

Her entire body tensed and she barely stopped herself from spinning around and screaming.

Kyle's hand fell to her shoulder. "Are you all right?"

She looked back at the spot where she saw those red eyes and, not surprisingly, they were no longer there. *Damn.*

"Yeah. I'm fine."

He turned her to face him, his gaze searching her face. "Are you sure? You went tense on me awful fast."

Emma took a deep breath to calm her nerves and immediately realized *that* had been a big mistake. Having Kyle this close to her, smelling so very nice, did nothing for her composure.

Maybe she simply needed to admit she wanted the man. A lot. And if she were like the women in her coven, she would have had him by now. She wasn't them, though. She was Emma. Boring, plain, safe Emma. Christ knew that wouldn't change anytime soon, since it hadn't changed for thirty-one years.

"I'm fine, Deputy. Thanks," she tacked on for no particular reason. Emma moved to step around Kyle, but he stepped in front of her and blocked her path.

Confused, she stared up at him. "What?"

"Tell me, Emma. Did you dream last night?"

She blinked and lied. "Not that I remember."

"Did I mention, Emma, I can tell when you're lying?"

Unable to help herself, she raised an eyebrow in disbelief. "Is that right?"

"Yup. I sure can."

"I'm not lying," she calmly lied.

He stepped toward her and Emma immediately stepped back.

"I think you are."

Emma shrugged, even as she kept backing up and he kept moving forward. "You believe what you want to believe."

"I do."

Her back slamming into the wall behind her, Emma could only stare up at Kyle as he stood in front of her, blocking her way out with his big gorgeous body.

"Are you trying to intimidate me or something?" 'Cause it was kind of working.

Kyle shook his head. "No."

"So what are you doing?"

"I don't rightly know." He slipped his hand behind the back of her neck, his fingers massaging the tense muscles while holding her in place. "But I do know what I want to do."

Then he leaned forward, his eyes locked on her lips. Emma knew she should do something, but her brain took that moment to completely shut down on her. She ended up watching Kyle lean down until his lips were barely a breath away from hers.

"You gonna stop me, Emma?" he whispered softly, his lips barely touching hers.

Emma was confused. Hot, horny, and confused. She didn't know what he was talking about because she kept waiting for him to goddamn kiss her. "Stop what?" she finally asked.

Kyle grinned. "Good girl."

He kissed her and Emma realized she might be in the biggest trouble of her life.

She tasted the same now as she did in the dream—amazing. He coaxed her lips open with gentle swipes of his tongue, and she responded with a heartfelt groan. Her hands reached up, and one dug in his hair while the other gripped his shoulder. He used his free arm to pull her small body tight into his.

Her tongue shyly touched his and his knees almost buckled, because she went from shy and delicate to hot and demanding in seconds.

Kyle had finally begun to realize something about his little Emma Lucchesi. Although definitely shy and cautious, once you got past those walls she'd built up…Lord, you were in heaven.

Her fingers dug into his shoulder and hair while her tongue boldly stroked his. She wanted him. And Kyle was more than happy to accommodate her. If he could only maneuver her over to the bed. A bit small, but it would do to get this first time out of the way…

"And how's our Miss Emma today?" Dale Sahara asked, pushing through the door of Emma's hospital room.

Kyle pulled away from Emma, his fangs bursting from his gums as he snarled his displeasure at Dale. "*Get. Out.*"

"All righty then," Sahara said, turning right around and walking back out.

Realizing his fangs were out, Kyle hugged Emma to his body, his chin resting against the top of her head. It took much to get the cat in him leashed.

He didn't know what this woman had done to him, but he knew he had to get himself under control. She was human. A human who wasn't staying. Flash his fangs or his claws, and he'd have a very big problem on his hands.

"I'm sorry, Emma," he whispered into her hair, barely forcing his fangs back.

Those hands that had gripped him like her life depended on it moments before now landed on his shoulders to push him away.

"Don't apologize," she said. But she wouldn't look at him. "It's not a big deal."

She tried to walk around him, but he grabbed her arm and turned her to face him.

"What's going on?"

Still without looking at him, using her hair to hide her face, she said, "Nothing."

"Don't play this game with me, Emma." He tipped her chin up with his knuckle. "Tell me what's going on."

She blinked once, and then she lied. "I gotta pee. Is that okay with you, Deputy?"

He couldn't exactly argue with her on that one, so he released her. She didn't run like he thought she might. Instead she walked away from him, throwing over her shoulder, casual as you please, "When I come out, you won't be here anymore."

The quiet closing of that bathroom door sure did sound mighty final.

SEVEN

"I have no idea what I did, but I screwed it up somehow."

"Maybe you should have kept those lips to yourself, big brother," Katie Treharne-MacClancy teasingly chastised. "You know those weak, full-human women can't handle the mighty men of Smithville."

"You come up with the biggest load of—"

"Besides," she cut in, "maybe you took her by surprise. You should try again."

"Nah. She made it clear she doesn't want me trying anything again."

"I'm sorry, Kyle." And she meant it. That's why he loved his baby sister. She got the best of both cat and dog emotionally and was a gorgeous woman. Unfortunately, her shifted self had not been so lucky. Funny-looking didn't quite describe the awkward mix of cat and canine his parents had forced upon his poor baby sister. Especially her snagglefang. The snagglefang broke his heart and made him laugh at the same time.

As a deputy, however, no one dared push his Kit-Kat past her tolerance point. Unlike her brothers, she put up with a lot more, and the town loved her for it. Unlike her brothers, however, when Katie snapped...well, it was never pretty, although he and Tully often found it damn entertaining.

"Don't be sorry, Kit-Kat. It isn't your fault. It's *his* fault."

"Who?"

"His. That big, shaggy-haired, interrupting bastard."

Katie laughed. "Do you mean Dale?"

"If it hadn't been for that lazy, twenty-hour-sleeping son of a bitch, I wouldn't have to spend the night in this goddamn SUV." He moved around again, trying to get comfortable in the front seat.

"That seems a little unfair, big brother."

Kyle had to spend the night in his SUV, staring at a dark hospital and hoping Emma would walk by her room window every once in a while. As far as he was concerned, *that* was the only unfair thing here.

"The man's an asshole."

"Kyle Treharne! You stop that." But he could hear his sister trying desperately not to laugh. "Now, if I were you, I'd go back in there and show that Yankee what a nice Southern boy can do for a gal."

"I better not, Kit-Kat. Getting involved with a full-human who doesn't plan on staying? A very bad idea."

"How do you know she won't stay? Maybe she'll stay for you."

"I've barely known the woman five minutes."

"And?"

"What do you mean, and?"

"I mean, maybe she's the one for you, if you'd stop being a gawd-darn cat for two seconds."

His sister always wanted to believe in love at first sight. Shame Kyle and Tully knew better.

"Oh, yeah. I'm sure when she finds me eating a whole deer on my dining room table, she'll say, 'Well hey, pretty kitty. Make sure to save me some.'"

Katie sighed, long and loud. "Kyle—"

"Forget it, Kit-Kat. I'll just keep my dumb hick ass out here. And leave her adorable Yankee ass in there. Then tomorrow, I'll send her on her way."

"As always, you're as hardheaded as Daddy. But, and I'll leave you with this, Kyle, 'cause I gotta go kick a little hyena ass downtown, there are more than one or two humans who live in this town, and they seem quite happy with their mates. Definitely happier than your miserable cat ass. But don't worry, darlin', I say that with love."

Laughing, Kyle hung up the phone.

True enough, there were full-humans mated to shifters, but that was rare and most of those full-humans were more animal than human in their soul. Whether it was in the way they moved or lived, they were comfortable with both sides of their mates.

Emma didn't seem comfortable with much of anything, so Kyle didn't really expect her to understand or accept what he was and always would be. No, he was better off waiting for the right leopard to come walking through his door. He needed a predator in his bed. A female who could handle a Pride of lions running by her front door in the morning and not start screaming when Tully showed up covered in blood, his Pack in tow, looking for cold beer and some of their momma's key lime pie.

Knowing he'd made the best decision, Kyle settled back in his SUV, very glad he'd run home and put on his sweats so he could be comfortable. Because it would definitely be a long, lonely night.

He didn't come back. Not that she wanted him to, but... he didn't come back.

You threw him out, you idiot.

What was she supposed to do?

Toss his fine ass on the bed and fuck him within an inch of his gorgeous life?

Oh, yeah. Sure. Rolling her eyes in annoyance, Emma tossed the magazine against the opposite wall as lightning outside her window lit up the entire room.

She jumped from the explosion and sighed when the hospital's electricity went out. *How could they not have a generator?* Or maybe they did and it wasn't working. But why wouldn't it?

Taking a deep breath to calm the warning bells screaming through her system, Emma used the lightning outside her room to illuminate her way to the window. More lightning flashed by, and even in her current state Emma had to admit how beautiful the natural power of the goddesses could be. This was where they ruled, and this was where some of the energy and power that her coven tapped into came from.

Emma placed her hand against the glass, fingers spread out, palm flat. She focused her thoughts, her energy, and called down the lightning. Multiple strikes slammed into the ground outside her window, moving closer and closer to her as her spell gained momentum. Then, when it got close enough, Emma called a strike right to her. It hit the glass, sending electricity through it and into her. Emma gritted her teeth and reveled in the feel of the Dark Mothers moving through her. She lifted her hand and watched white sparks flicker between her fingers.

With another deep breath, she centered herself. Focusing all her energy and strength, streaming it, making it even more powerful. Then Emma spun around, unleashing that lightning on the thing that had just launched itself at her back.

The thing that had already tried to kill her once.

Its black, filth-encrusted fur sizzled as its body flipped back and slammed into the opposite wall. It moved and, in a panic, Emma hit it again with the remaining energy in her body.

It twitched and Emma jumped. Good gods, the thing wasn't dead. After all that, it wasn't dead.

It blocked the door to the hall, so she ran for the bathroom, slamming the door as the beast crashed into it. Anything natural or from this plane of existence would have disintegrated instantly from all the lightning she'd poured into it. Instead, this thing still fought even while its unholy body dissolved around it.

Unholy. Unnatural. Goddess, did they actually do this? Did her Coven conjure this thing?

She couldn't worry about that now. Not when it kept throwing itself against the door, trying to get in. She knew that it would try to kill her until it took its last breath.

Emma only had one way out and she took it, scrambling up onto the toilet and pushing the lone window open. Shoving herself through, she slipped on the toilet lid, and suddenly Emma had the ground rushing up to meet her as she tumbled out—head first.

He'd been seconds away from contacting the Water & Power guys to tell them the generator at the hospital had failed again when he saw the vicious lightning strike slam right outside Emma's window and then ricochet up, slamming through the glass and into the hand Emma had pressed against it.

Kyle was already moving when he saw Emma turn, faster than he'd ever seen her move. In fact, he didn't know humans could move like that.

That's when he saw it. Some kind of big black dog stood behind her. Kyle had never seen it before. It wasn't local. To be quite honest, he didn't know what the hell that thing was. He only knew it moved on Emma with unholy speed. But she used the lightning she'd pulled into her body and slammed the thing back away from her—twice. Then Emma ran. Not out the door, but into the bathroom.

Kyle changed direction and went around the hospital. He found Emma tumbling out the window, head first, as the thing inside her room raged and slammed into the bathroom door, nearly taking it off its hinges.

Sliding under the window, Kyle caught Emma in his arms before she hit hard, pain-inducing earth.

She screamed, fighting him.

"Emma! It's me!"

Those brown eyes of hers looked up in shock. Then her small hands grabbed his shoulders.

"We've gotta—"

"I know, darlin'." He placed her on her feet. "Move."

He didn't have to tell her twice. She took off running, heading around the hospital building.

"Get in!" he yelled over the storm that seemed to have worsened in the last three minutes. Emma pulled the passenger side door open and scrambled into the front seat. Kyle got in and slammed his door, turning the key he'd left in the ignition. The SUV rumbled to life and Kyle pulled out onto the road. Emma looked through her window, then she kneeled on the seat, her knees pushing into the leather.

"It's behind us."

"It won't be for long. Buckle up, darlin'."

She did as he ordered and once she was securely belted in, he made a wild turn into the woods. One small hand gripped the armrest between the seats while the other gripped the handle over the door that Tully always called the "oh shit!" bar.

Emma didn't say anything, which Kyle appreciated.

He made a few more wild turns, knowing he couldn't stop until he heard it. Knowing he wasn't safe until he heard it.

As soon as he'd stepped out of his truck to get Emma, he'd sensed them heading toward the hospital. They'd known an outsider had come to their town. Not sweet little Emma but something else. Something they'd have to kill.

Now that he had Emma, Kyle knew some of them would split off to protect his back while others would continue on to track and kill that thing. So when he heard it over the driving rain, he breathed a sigh of relief.

Tully's howl. Calming him as it never had before.

A roar answered Tully's howl. A loud lion roar. Followed by another roar. The roar of bears.

Kyle slowed down his truck and passed through two boulders leading to his house. On top of it stood Tully, his small hoop earring glinting as lightning flashed nearby.

He nodded at Kyle, his wolf head dipping just a bit to let Kyle know they were watching out for him and that Emma would be safe.

Because at the moment, that's all Kyle really cared about.

EIGHT

Emma didn't look at Kyle when he pulled the passenger side door open. She couldn't. Instead she sat in his SUV, her entire body shaking. Not from fear, although she was woman enough to admit she was scared shitless, but from shame. What if her Coven *had* done this? What if, in their quest for power, they'd unleashed this thing on Smithville? They'd put all these people in danger. Bear. Tully. Dr. Sahara.

Kyle.

"Come on, Emma."

Strong arms slipped under her knees and her back, easily lifting her out. A few steps took them to the porch of a small house while he tried his best to protect her from the rain with his body.

He carried her up the stairs and pushed the door open. Without a key.

She nearly moaned in despair. Kyle, who didn't exactly seem to be much of a trusting fellow, felt comfortable enough in his town to leave his door unlocked for hours at a time.

Kyle stepped into his house, reaching over to flip a switch. No lights came on, and he sighed. "Electricity's out here, too."

He released Emma's legs and slowly lowered her to the ground. "Wait here." Gentle fingers brushed against her cheek, and he disappeared into the darkness.

SHELLY LAURENSTON

She shouldn't stay. She should leave. She was putting Kyle in danger, and she'd never forgive herself if something happened. "Kyle, maybe I should—"

"Don't even think about leaving," his deep voice replied from the darkness as he easily moved around the house with absolutely no light to see by.

She really hated when he got that tone. "Look, I'm just trying to protect your egotistical ass. It's not safe for me to be here."

"I don't need your protection. And you couldn't be safer."

Emma looked at the open door and wondered about making a run for it. Then she heard the howling.

"Wh...what was that?" Was it that thing coming for her?

"Wolves. Nothing to worry about."

"Are you sure?"

"Very."

"Aren't they dangerous? I thought they were...uh, predators or something."

"They like to think so, but I consider them more scavengers myself."

After several moments, a match flared and met paper. The fireplace burned to life, and Emma looked at the room she stood in for the first time.

"Wow," she muttered as she examined what she could see. "This is really cute."

Kyle stood and walked over to her. "Cute? I wasn't going for cute, darlin'. I was going for rugged and manly."

This didn't surprise Emma. All made from highly polished and gorgeously put-together wood, the floors, ceiling, and furniture looked as if they could handle any abuse. One big picture window looked out over the forest surrounding Kyle's property, with smaller windows dotting the rest of the house. Not a big place at all, with the living room flowing into the dining room, which flowed right into the kitchen, a hallway led off, and she assumed that it led to Kyle's bedroom. The enormous couches and chairs were plush and begged her to stretch out and take a quick nap.

Yeah, this place wasn't big or fancy, but it was beautiful.

"Well…" she teased, trying to lighten a mood that could definitely turn sour, "you definitely managed cute."

Grinning, he stepped around her and closed the door. "You must be freezing."

"No. Just a little chilled." She stepped over to the fireplace and looked at the pictures that were on the mantel. The first one that grabbed her eye was the picture of Kyle with his arm around a young woman. Since it still was kind of dark, Emma leaned in closer, trying to get a good look without setting herself on fire by falling into the fireplace. Who the hell was this woman? And why the hell did Emma care?

"That's my baby sister," Kyle's voice announced in her ear.

Emma barely stopped herself from jumping out of her skin. The man moved without making a sound. She found it unsettling.

"Um…yeah. I can tell," she lied. "You two look alike."

"Actually, she looks more like Tully. She's our half-sister. Born after my parents got married."

"She's really cute."

"Yup."

Clearing her throat, Emma looked at the other pictures. "Wow," she exclaimed again. "Did you get this at a wildlife reserve or something?"

She took the picture off the mantel and crouched in front of the fireplace for a better look. She'd never seen anything like it. Two wolves. Two black panthers. And one... Her eyes squinted. *Jesus, what is that thing?* It kind of looked like a big cat, but its ears were weird and it had a bit of a snaggletooth problem. Whatever it was, they were all together. Practically snuggling. She'd never seen panthers and wolves "snuggle".

Kyle crouched next to her and smiled at the picture. "Reserve? Yeah, something like that."

"It's just... I've never seen these kinds of animals together in one picture. And this wolf looks like he's... posing?" She could almost hear it growling, "Cheese!"

Her eyes narrowed. "What's on that wolf's ear? Is that an earring?"

With an awkward laugh, Kyle took hold of the frame. "Yeah. Sure. Like a pirate dog." He stood and carefully placed the picture back on his mantel.

"So," he said, staring down at her, "you're a witch."

That wasn't really a question, now was it?

"Whatever gave you that idea?" She tried to make that sound light and airy, like Seneca would have. Of course, that girl could talk herself out of any situation. That's how they got out of hell. From what they knew, Satan still spoke of Sen kindly.

"What gave me that idea? I saw you manipulate lightning."

"Oh." She waved that away. "That's like juggling."

"Juggling? You expect me to believe that?"

With a deep sigh, Emma walked over to one of Kyle's couches and dropped onto it. "No. I don't expect you to believe it."

He crouched in front of her, his big fingers touching her cheek gently. "Then tell me what's going on, Emma."

NINE

Kyle reared back. "What do you mean, no?"

"I mean no. I'm not telling you anything."

"Why the hell not?"

Emma stood and walked around him. "Because it's none of your business."

"It is now."

Rubbing her hands over her face, she said, "Kyle... don't make this difficult."

She hadn't called him by his first name since that hot dream. He liked when she said his name. Even when she snarled it.

"Emma, I wish you would trust me."

"You don't trust me."

He cringed inside and worried about where this might be going. "What do you mean?"

"Oh, come on." She turned around and faced him. "Do I look stupid to you?"

"No, but—"

"I know what's going on."

"You do?"

"Yeah." She raised herself on her toes so she could look him squarely in the neck. "Government. Experiment."

It took him a second, but when he laughed in her face... no, she didn't take that well at all.

"I'm leaving."

"And going where?" he demanded as she snatched open the front door. And just as quickly she closed it again.

"There's a wolf in front of your porch."

Kyle cleared his throat. "Yeah?"

Her eyes narrowed and she growled between clenched teeth, "Government. Experiment."

"This is not a government experiment. It's the South. There's a lot of nature and ... stuff around."

"Nature and stuff?" Nope. She didn't sound like she believed him at all. "Do I look like an idiot to you?"

"Of course not."

Kyle's phone went off, and he snatched it off his jeans.

Emma held her hand out. "That's for me."

Now Kyle narrowed his eyes and answered. "Hello?"

"Hello. Can I speak to Emma, please?" said a female voice.

He handed the phone over and Emma took it from his hand and walked out of the room. The bathroom door slammed shut, and he was about to go over there and shove it open, since he had no locks on his doors anyway, when his landline rang.

"Yeah?"

"Hey, big brother."

Kyle smiled. "Kit-Kat. What's up, darlin'?"

"Bear wanted me to let you know everything's okay. That thing ... at the hospital. She fried it."

"But it was still fighting. It came after us."

"It did," his sister agreed. "Until I took a shovel to its head. Again and again and again. Then it stopped fighting completely. Miss Sophie and Miss Addie are heading over here now to deal with the remains, which I have to say ... smell damn funky."

Kyle's smile turned into a grin. He absolutely loved his baby sister.

"Aren't you just the handy girl."

"I am. Now the question is, are you all right? Heard you were the white knight and rescued our little Miss Emma."

"Something like that."

"Well, you can tell her the coast is clear."

Kyle frowned. He knew if he told Emma that, she'd leave. And he didn't want her to. "Maybe. Sure. But she isn't feeling real friendly at the moment."

Katie took a deep breath. "Kyle, I've heard rumors."

"What rumors?"

"Well, I'm sure you've figured out she's a witch."

"Duh."

"The Coven and the Elders are fighting it out. The Coven wants your little helpless victim and her coven to take over for them."

"She's hardly helpless. And what do the Elders have to do with who takes over and who doesn't?"

"That's what I was thinking. But it turns out that this new coven don't worship that wood nymph goddess. Artie something?"

Kyle rolled his eyes. "Artemis?"

"Yeah. Her."

"You never did pay attention in mythology class."

"Boring. Anyway, they apparently worship the darker goddesses. Which I find damn fascinating."

Of course she did. Katie loved trouble.

"The Elders aren't happy, but the Coven is standing firm."

"All right. Thanks for letting me know what's going on."

"You going to tell her the truth?"

"What truth?"

"About why this town needs a coven."

"No. That's not my responsibility."

"Kyle—"

"No. 'Cause to be honest, baby sister, I don't think she has any intention of staying. And it'll be a cold day in hell when I tell a Yankee anything that could put my town at risk."

"Suit yourself. But Tully says you like her."

"You and Tully mind your own damn business."

"Fine. Be that way." His sister hung up the phone, and Kyle sighed.

Damn family.

"Why did I suddenly roll out of bed?"

Emma closed the bathroom door. "Bad dreams?"

"Emma."

"Okay. Okay. That thing that tried to kill me. It tried again. I think I got it, but I had to pull some mighty power to make it happen."

"What did you use?"

"Lightning."

"Ooh. Using nature. Good move." Jamie could be entertained by the strangest things.

"I don't know if I killed it, though. And I don't know if we conjured that thing."

"How bad is this?"

Emma took a breath. "I'd say not that bad 'cause I know we could handle it, except for one thing."

"Which is?"

"Another coven. An older one. Living here. Came to the hospital to check me out. And I don't know why."

"Maybe they wanted to make sure you wouldn't be any trouble. You know, protecting their town."

"Maybe. Only it didn't feel that way. I'd swear they were expecting me."

"Really?" She could hear the interest in Jamie's voice. "I'm not liking the sound of that, sweetie."

Cringing, Emma said, "You're coming down here, aren't you?"

"What do you think?"

Emma thought about it a moment, then nodded. "It's probably for the best. Even if I killed this thing, Jamie, we need to make sure there's no more."

"You're worried about that little town."

"It's a nice place. Weird. But nice. If we unleashed something here...we have to clean it up. We have to fix it."

"We will. I promise. Look for us tomorrow. We'll be there."

"I know you will."

"Are you okay?"

Emma closed her eyes. "I feel raw. Angry."

"It's all that power you used, combined with the fear. What you're feeling is normal. It'll dissipate."

"When? 'Cause I don't like it."

"Hard to tell. Jogging helps, though. Or sometimes I do yoga."

"Yoga? Did you just recommend yoga to me?" Even as she said the words, Emma could hear herself getting louder and could feel more anger than she normally ever had to deal with bubbling up inside her.

"Uh...Em?"

"Is there anything about me that says I like to twist myself into a pretzel? Seriously. Because I'd like to know."

"Well, sweetie, it was just a suggestion."

"A *stupid* suggestion."

"Okay. On that note, I'm going to let you go get some rest or something before we get into a really ugly fight and hex each other over the phone."

"Fine. Whatever." Emma slapped the phone closed and tried to get control of her running emotions. Tomorrow she'd have to apologize to Jamie, but at the moment, if the woman happened to be standing right in front of her, Emma felt pretty confident she'd punch her lights out.

Liking the idea way more than she should, Emma snatched the bathroom door open to find Kyle standing there.

And that's when she absolutely lost it.

Emma pushed past Kyle and stormed back into the living room. "Were you listening to my phone conversation?"

"No," he answered honestly. "I wanted to see if you were hungry. Or if you needed some dry clothes."

She spun on him and threw his phone right at his chest. "Don't lie to me!"

Kyle took a deep breath. "Emma, I know you've had a long night."

"Yeah. And?"

"So maybe you should calm down."

Emma marched up to him, her small but surprisingly strong forefinger slamming into his chest, punctuating each word she spoke. "Don't. Tell. Me. To. Calm. *Down!*"

"Don't yell at me, and stop poking me with that damn tiny finger."

Emma's eye twitched, and Kyle watched as she took her forefinger and slowly moved it toward his chest.

What the hell is she doing?

After what seemed like hours, Emma's small finger poked his chest. Hard.

Kyle lightly slapped her hand away, getting good and pissed off himself. "Stop it, Emma."

She poked him again.

"I said stop it."

And again. "If it's annoying you so much"—and again—"then stop me your damn self."

And again.

Like that, Kyle's control snapped like dry wood during a summer heat wave.

Without thought, only animal instinct, he grabbed hold of Emma's hand and yanked her close. She gave a startled gasp but said nothing else. He needed her to say "Stop." He needed her to say it before it didn't matter what the hell she said.

Instead, she looked up at him, her lips slightly parted.

"Emma." He growled her name. Snarled it. She didn't run. Didn't try and pull away. No. Instead, the crazy little Yankee raised herself the smallest bit on her toes, her eyes staring straight at his mouth.

"Damn it!" was the last thing he said before he claimed her mouth with his. Like everything else about their relationship, even their kiss was a fight. Their tongues sparred for dominance while Emma pushed that soft little body against his and wrapped her arms around his neck.

The last thing his rational mind thought or, in this case, prayed, "Please, Lord. Don't let her change her mind."

Asshole, asshole, asshole. Kyle Treharne was such an asshole. Didn't stop her from wanting him, though. She wanted the man more than she'd ever wanted anything before in her life.

She especially wanted him like this. Kind of wild and out of control. Emma had never had a guy treat her like he couldn't wait to fuck her. She'd always had polite, kind sex with polite, kind guys who acted like they couldn't wait for her to meet their mother. Taking her to bed seemed perfunctory, not something they had to do before they lost their minds.

Kyle pulled out of their kiss with an angry snarl that should have had her running back out into the storm. Instead, she worried he might be trying to bail on her. He pushed her back several feet until the back of her legs hit the couch. With one shove, she landed on the big sectional. Before she had a chance to get back up, he was on top of her, his mouth devouring hers, his hands damn near everywhere on her body. She felt completely naked but she still wore her wet oversized sweats.

Big hands slipped under her sweatshirt, pushing the thick cotton up until her breasts were exposed. Never really needing a bra before anyway, she'd decided to forgo one during her hospital stay. Kind of Emma's way of running wild. So worth it, if Kyle's groan of appreciation told her anything.

His mouth skimmed across her upper chest, his rough tongue leaving a wet trail along her heated flesh. The tip of Kyle's nose tickled her already-hard nipples and she couldn't help but giggle. Then he sucked one into his so-warm mouth and Emma gasped, her back arching, pushing her closer to him. Her hands, originally gripping the arm of the couch, now gripped the back of Kyle's head, forcing him closer to her, demanding what he seemed more than ready to give.

A rumbling purr resonated from him and right into her, setting her entire body on fire. She wrapped her legs around Kyle's waist and her hips pushed against his like he was already fucking her. Like he was already inside of her, buried deep.

Releasing one breast, he leaned up and kissed her again, stopping only to pull her sweatshirt completely off. Then he went to her other breast, and Emma wondered exactly how much more she could take. Her need to come was nearly wiping out her sanity, and yet he kept playing with her.

He slid his fingers down her stomach, under the sweatpants, and under her panties. Two fingers pushed inside her, and Emma cried out, clinging to him tighter, one hand still digging into his scalp, the other leaving nail marks in his shoulder.

His fingers fucked her hard, not remotely gentle. And she didn't want him to be. She wanted him to fuck her so hard she would scream his name and promise to buy him a Florida condo. She wanted the son of a bitch to fuck her raw. She knew he would, too.

"God, Kyle!"

Her plea ripped another growl from him, and he released her long enough to sit back on his haunches so he could pull down her sweatpants. He got them down as far as he needed them to be, then he reached for her.

She grabbed his hands and he snarled at her. "*What?*" His voice might sound like he was pissed off, but his light eyes were begging her not to stop him. Pleading.

"Con...condoms," she stammered out.

He blinked, like he'd suddenly come back into the room. Then he scrambled off her and disappeared into the blackness. She'd never seen a man move so fast—and, even more importantly, he was moving that fast for *her.*

Before she could even think about what she might be doing and if she should stop, Kyle was back. The box of condoms hit the floor right by the couch and then he landed on top of her again. He kissed and licked her neck, then he bit it.

Emma whimpered and clung to Kyle. A few more seconds and she'd start begging. A few more seconds and she'd promise the man absolutely *anything.*

Kyle could smell her lust for him, and it pushed him past the point of being human. His cat side took over his human body with every intention of having the hot little thing desperately pushing his sweatpants down.

Naked and warm and so wet Kyle thought both his heads might explode, this little gal had brought out a side of him he'd always had under serious control.

With only a touch and a kiss, this woman had ripped away all of that, leaving the raw animal behind.

His sweats pushed down *enough*, Kyle slammed that stupid condom on and shoved her back down to the couch, moving over her. The last remnants of his human self yelled at him to slow down, to take it easy, but he couldn't. Especially when she reached for his cock with both hands while spreading her legs wide. Her pussy glistened at him in the firelight, and he snarled.

Before her hands could get a firm grip, he grabbed her wrists and pushed them above her head, pinning her to the spot and reminding him of that wonderful dream. He placed the tip of his cock against her wet slit, and while they both watched, he shoved into her hard.

"Damn!" he groaned.

"God!" she screamed.

He stopped. Lord, he didn't want to hurt her. But she looked at him with such horror, he did all he could to rein himself in. Until she said, "*What... what are you doing?*" She fought the hands holding her down.

Kyle looked down into her face, where the beginning of tears filled her eyes. He knew then he had to let her go. He wouldn't hurt Emma. Not for anything.

Then she said, "Please, Kyle. *Please.*" He stared at her, and suddenly he realized what he was seeing. Not pain or fear…but hunger. Hunger for him. The same hunger he had for her. They wanted the same thing, the same way.

That was all he needed to know.

Releasing her arms, Kyle ordered, "Grab your knees, darlin', and lift 'em."

After one startled look, she did what he ordered and wrapped her hands around her knees, lifting them up so her thighs cradled his hips. He placed his hands on either side of her chest.

Staring down at her, he prayed his fangs wouldn't come out. "Hold on."

With that, he drove into her as hard as he wanted to. Emma screamed, her back arching, her fingers gripping her knees tighter. He slammed into her again and again. By the fourth stroke she was coming, and he wasn't nearly done.

Emma couldn't have stopped that orgasm if she tried. Never in her life had she been fucked so hard, and wow…did it rock, or what? She pulled her knees higher, allowing him deeper inside her body, and her orgasm simply kept rolling along.

"Look at me, Emma."

She didn't realize she'd closed her eyes and had turned her head away until he said that. Emma looked into Kyle's face, and another wave slammed into her.

No one had ever looked at her like that. No one.

"That's right, darlin'," he groaned. "That's right."

His hips pistoned against hers, pushing his hard and oh-so-large cock inside her again and again. She felt ripped from the inside out, and goddamn, but nothing had ever felt so fucking good before.

"Again," he ordered. "Come for me again."

Oh, he must be joking. She shook her head no, unable to speak the word.

"Again, Emma. Now."

It was like the bastard owned her body. And maybe, at the moment anyway, he did. That was the only way she could explain how he managed to pump another blinding climax out of her. This one stronger and more powerful than the last.

"Oh, yeah, darlin'. Yeah." Then his back arched and he came, his body shaking as he exploded inside her. He pumped his hips two more times before crash-landing right on top of her.

And Emma only had one question on her mind as her body worked to recover ...

Did he just hiss at me?

TEN

He had to get off her. He really did. But still...she was so warm and soft. And he was so damn comfortable.

"Can't breathe."

Damn.

By sheer force of will, Kyle pushed himself up and off Emma, throwing himself back so he rested against the opposite end of the couch.

Breathing hard, their sweatpants down around their ankles, the two stared at each other for what felt like hours as opposed to the few seconds it actually turned out to be.

Then Kyle watched, fascinated, as Emma grabbed hold of the sofa pillow and covered her pretty, sweat-drenched face with it. There she was...Painfully Shy Emma. He had to admit, she was just as dang cute as Demanding, Bitchy Emma.

"I can't believe I did that," she groaned. "I want us to be clear"—she peeked over the pillow—"I do not do this often or anything."

Kyle nodded. "I could tell."

Emma slammed the pillow down onto her lap, covering up that pretty little pussy. "What the hell does that mean?"

Okay, exactly when did this conversation go wrong? How did he manage to do that so easily with her?

She struggled to sit up, but her body was not exactly cooperating. "Well?"

Shrugging, he told her, "Darlin', you were a little too tight to be well used."

Clearly confused, she stared at him. "Huh?"

Unable to feel stressed about anything, Kyle sighed out, "Your pussy, sweetheart." He stretched against the couch like the big satisfied cat he was at the moment and smiled. "Tight and perfect."

A small grin turned up the corners of her mouth. "Oh. Well, thanks... I guess."

They stared at each other for a moment and then, with a tiny squeak, she covered up her face again with the pillow and turned her entire body away like she was trying to curl into herself.

Lord, if it wasn't her hair hiding that face, it was a damn pillow.

"What now?"

"Nothing," she mumbled into the pillow.

Still too mellow to worry about much of anything, he removed the condom and wiped himself off with a tissue before dumping it all in the trash can right next to the couch. With another too-relaxed sigh, Kyle leaned his head back against the armrest and stared up at the ceiling. He and his brother had built this house together, with his sister occasionally stepping in to cause additional problems. They did a nice job and only got into five or ten actual fistfights over the two years it took.

Emma moved and he knew—*knew*—she was going to run out on him. Even if she had to brave that nightmare storm to do it.

He slammed his foot down onto the lowered sweatpants she'd been desperately trying to pull back up and locked his sights on her face.

"Eep!" At least that's what it sounded like she said.

"What are you doing?"

"Um … I … uh …"

"You weren't thinking about leaving, were you?"

"Well … ya know …"

"'Cause you're not going anywhere."

"Well, I don't want to put you out or anything. I can stay at a hotel or—"

"We ain't done, Emma."

Her entire body tensed at his words, and her small hands grabbed tight hold of that damn pillow again. "No?"

"No." Not remotely done.

"Oh. Okay."

She looked away, unable to meet his eyes. No. This wouldn't do. He didn't want to deal with Painfully Shy Emma when it came to sex. He wanted the ballbuster. He wanted the woman who wouldn't let him get away with a goddamn thing.

"Come here," he ordered.

"Uh …"

"Now, Emma."

"Stop ordering me around. It's annoying the hell outta me." Ahhh. There she was—his little ballbuster.

"Come here, Emma," he coaxed, "and I'll make it worth your while."

Her lip caught between her teeth.

"Don't make me wait, darlin'. I hate that."

Using her hands, she pushed herself up until she rested on her knees. She moved forward and he shook his head. "Leave the pillow."

Emma actually looked down at it like he'd asked her to leave her oxygen tank behind while going underwater. Eventually, though, she dropped it and moved forward again.

"Wait."

She sighed in frustration. "What?"

"Take the sweatpants off. I want you naked."

"Oh." With less hesitation, she shimmied out of her sweatpants. Watching made his cock hard again, and her eyes widened when she noticed.

"Now, come here."

She shuffled over to him on her knees while he pulled his sweatshirt off and tossed it across the room. By the time she reached him, he'd kicked the pants off and slipped another condom on.

"Can you handle another ride?"

With a chuckle, she looked away from his direct gaze. "The way you talk is…uh…interesting. Most of the guys from my neighborhood just say, 'You wanna fuck again or what?'"

"Don't compare me to Yankees, and you didn't answer my question."

Emma's nipples stiffened and she gave a small nod, her eyes focused intently on his cock.

"A hard one?" he pushed, enjoying the blush creeping over her entire body.

"Yeah. Sure." She swallowed and licked her lips, her big brown eyes still locked on his cock like she couldn't wait to get to it. "Why not?" she asked *it* as opposed to asking him.

"Then bring that pretty little ass over here."

Emma crawled into his lap and he held his cock, wordlessly telling her to impale herself on it. She did, slowly, and they both groaned at the contact.

Once he had her right where he wanted her, Kyle reached up and did what he'd been aching to do since he met her—he pushed her hair off her face. She pulled back a bit, but he wouldn't let her go. Instead, he pulled her down for a kiss while keeping her hair off her face. First, he'd fuck her again. Then he'd fuck her in the shower. Both would involve getting her hair wet—sweat from the workout and water from the shower—so he could easily comb it out of his way to get a good long look at that pretty face.

"It's gonna be slower this time, Emma," he said between kisses.

"Okay,"

"Harder, too."

Fresh, hot wetness coated his latex-covered cock, and she panted. Her hands reached up and gripped his biceps, her fingers digging into the skin.

"You up for that, Little Emma?"

She groaned and said, "Are you going to keep asking me questions, or are you going to get to it?"

"Anything you want, darlin'. Absolutely anything." And then he gave her exactly what she wanted for the rest of the night.

Eleven

All night. They'd gone at it all night.

She'd heard about having sex all night but all her—few—past boyfriends usually passed out by one or two in the morning. Not Kyle. He kept going until about seven when, while showering together—which involved him licking her clean from head to toe—she finally begged him to let her sleep.

Five hours later and she had the overwhelming desire to make a run for it. Especially since she had no idea where Kyle was at the moment. She didn't want any uncomfortable morning-after conversations. She really didn't want any "pauses."

Without bothering to think about it too much, she slipped out of bed intent on finding her clothes, but she froze when she saw the big window above Kyle's bed. With the sun shining bright she could see a sparse forest with lots of tall trees taking up most of the view, but off to her right she could see the beach. The man had an ocean view. She used to dream about having a house with an ocean view, but on Long Island she'd need a few million to make that happen.

Shaking her head at the distraction, Emma remembered her clothes were still on the living-room floor.

"Shit, shit, shit," she muttered to herself while quietly stepping out into the hallway. She looked around and didn't see Kyle. So, moving quickly and silently, she tiptoed down the hall and through the living room. Her clothes littered the floor and she grabbed at them, piling them in her arms.

She tiptoed over to the front door and pulled it open. Bright sunlight nearly blinded her, and the sound of the close-by ocean filled the house. *I love it*, she thought, a split second of regret cutting through her.

She shook her head. *No feeling sorry for yourself.* She'd get dressed, head back to the hospital and get her stuff, then get a hotel room at that Smithville Arms place. By tomorrow morning, she'd be on a plane back home with her Coven and that would be that.

Nodding her head, she took a step out the door.

"Now, did I tell you to get dressed, darlin'?"

Emma turned and slammed right into Kyle's chest. She never heard him come up behind her. She didn't even realize he'd been in the house, much less in the room. Wearing a pair of black sweatpants that rode low on his hips and nothing else, Kyle stared down at her.

And that's when Emma realized she was in deeper than she should be. Way deeper than she should be. Because nothing, absolutely *nothing*, had ever looked so damn beautiful as this man in sweatpants.

Before she could do something stupid—like throw herself at him and promise never-ending love and fidelity—Emma burst out in one quick rush, "I was thinking I should go back to the hospital or get a hotel room or something." So *that I can avoid this particular morning-after conversation as if my life depended on it.*

Kyle's light gold eyes watched her, like someone might size up a lobster in a tank for dinner.

"So you're just going to leave, Emma?" he finally said while gently pulling her back into the house. "Walk out on me?"

"I wouldn't put it that way."

Reaching around her, he slammed the door shut.

"Then what way would you put it?" he asked, his fingers sliding across her jaw and down her throat. Emma's toes curled against the hardwood floor. "You had your fun and now you're going to go sneaking out on me?"

Was he kidding? "It's not like that."

Slowly, Kyle moved in on her, and Emma moved back and around as he maneuvered her away from the door. "My momma warned me about city women like you."

Emma clutched her clothes to her chest as she stumbled away from him. "Actually... Long Island is more of a suburb."

"She said y'all come down here for some good-ol'-boy lovin' and then you leave us. Alone... and broken."

A rather unladylike snort burst out of her, and Kyle sighed. "Now you're laughing at me?"

"I'm not laughing at you. I just..." She watched as Kyle took hold of her sweatshirt with two fingers and tossed it over his shoulder. "Look, Kyle—" And there went her sweatpants.

Emma's ass slammed into something hard, and she turned to find the dining-room table behind her. *Uh-oh.*

"I won't be tossed aside, Emma. Used for my body."

She turned and slapped her hands against his chest. "Stop it. Right now," she demanded, even while she laughed. Even while she squirmed.

"We're not done, Emma."

"We have to be."

Kyle shook his head, his disheveled black hair falling in front of his eyes. "Nope. Sorry. Can't do it."

"What do you mean you can't—hey!" How she ended up flat on her back on that dining-room table, she had no idea.

Kyle threw her legs over his shoulders and licked the inside of her thigh. "Come on, darlin'," he teased. "Give it up to ol' Kyle."

"You start referring to yourself in third person and we are so going to have a problem."

"Okay. I'll stop. But only if you promise to spend the day with me." He grinned at her. "Ya know, so I don't feel so used."

"Okay. If you're—oh!"

Before she could finish her sentence, Kyle pushed her legs against her chest and leaned down. He brushed his mouth against her pussy, and she whimpered.

"You're already so wet, Emma." He looked up at her, and she didn't quite know what to do with the heat she saw in that handsome face. And all of it for her, apparently. "Have you been thinking about me this morning?"

Had she been thinking of anything else?

She nodded, not sure she should risk speaking.

"Did you touch yourself while you were? Did you make yourself come?"

"I haven't done that with my hands since I gave myself carpal tunnel a couple of years ago."

He stood there for a second, his mouth so close to her clit she thought she might burst out of her skin if he didn't touch it, or stroke it, or *something*. But then he started laughing. So hard, he finally laid his head on her stomach, his arms resting on the table.

Confused, she stared at him. Then her eyes widened and she said, "No, no! I got carpal tunnel from typing too much at my job!"

Kyle laughed harder. He hadn't laughed this much in a long time. And never with a female he'd been sleeping with.

Getting off and getting out being the way of most residents of Smithville, both male and female.

Emma, though...Emma was different. Being with her felt so good. He could relax, and not once did she try and go for his throat or try and take his deer. But in no way was she boring in bed. A little shy at times, but once he got her hot enough—which didn't take much—her shyness went right out the window.

"Come on, darlin'." He wiped tears from his eyes, then slipped his hands under her body and lifted her into his arms. "Let's take this to the bedroom."

She buried her face in his neck. "Good. I need a pillow."

Kyle coughed to stop the laugh about to come out. "Don't be embarrassed, Emma." He wrapped her legs around his waist and headed to his bedroom. "You can say whatever you want to me. Don't forget that."

"And you won't laugh?"

"No. I'll probably laugh, but it'll be with love."

"Gee, thanks, Kyle."

He laid her gently on the bed and stretched out with her. "Now, darlin', don't be mad." His cell phone rang and he snarled. "I'm not answering that."

Kyle leaned in to kiss her and Emma put her hand over his face. "Aren't you supposed to be protecting and serving?"

"Emma—"

"You have to answer the phone, Kyle. What if there's a big bank heist or something?"

He laughed again, hard, but she only stared at him and he realized she probably wouldn't get the joke.

With a sigh he said, "Fine. I'll answer the damn phone."

Reaching over, he grabbed his cell from the nightstand. "Yeah?"

"It's Bear. There's an Elder meeting in an hour."

"So?" Bear had to go to those on occasion, as did Tully, but even though Kyle's daddy was a member, they'd never asked Kyle to attend before.

"They want you there."

"Bear—"

"Did I make it sound like this was open for discussion? In an hour, cat."

Kyle snapped his phone closed and looked at the woman lying next to him. The *naked* woman lying next to him.

"You've gotta go?" She sounded half disappointed and half relieved.

"I have a meeting in an hour."

She started to sit up. "Then I better—"

He tossed the phone to the floor and laid his hand against the soft skin above her breasts. "What exactly led you to the conclusion you were to get up?"

"Christ, you are so damn bossy!"

"Yep."

"And it's really annoying."

"So I've heard." He leaned over and licked each nipple. She groaned and he smiled. "An hour, Emma. We've got an hour to play." He gave her a light push back to the mattress. "So keep that adorable ass right where it is till I'm done with it."

TWELVE

Emma stepped out of Kyle's SUV and closed the door, but she leaned back through the open window.

"I'll be fine. I don't need you babysitting me."

Kyle frowned, looking around at the nearly deserted streets. "Are you sure you wouldn't rather wait at the house?"

"Yeah. I'm sure. I'm just going to get some breakfast, or it might be more of a brunch."

"All right." That frown on his face seemed to be getting worse and worse, but she had no idea why. "But don't go wandering around without me."

"Why?"

He stared at her. "Why what?"

"Why don't you want me wandering around without you?"

"You ask a lot of damn questions."

"Yeah, and you never answer them."

Quiet for a long moment, staring off down the street, Kyle seemed to finally come to some conclusion, "Tonight."

"Tonight what?"

"Tonight I'll answer your questions. Tonight I'll tell you anything you want to know."

"O ... kay."

"Don't panic on me yet."

"Government experiment," she whispered.

Kyle's frown deepened even more. "Again with that?"

She shook her head. "Forget it."

"Good. Now come here and kiss me."

Chuckling, Emma lifted herself up so she hung half in and half out of his SUV window. Kyle leaned across the seats and kissed her, his mouth warm and delicious. She loved how he kissed her. Like he actually enjoyed it. Like he could do it for hours if she let him. Which was why it took her a good twenty seconds to realize he was slowly pulling her back into the SUV.

"Oh, no." She pulled away laughing. "I'm hungry..." His eyebrow peaked. "For food!"

"Fine. Be that way."

"I will." She again stood safely on the outside of the SUV. "Go to your meeting, you're already late."

"All right. You got my cell phone?" She held the small black device up. He'd handed it to her and told her to use Tully's number to contact him. "Call me if you need me. Okay?"

She knew he meant it, and that felt really nice. She nodded. "I will."

Before Kyle walked into the Smithville Junior High classroom where the Elders held their monthly meetings, he felt damn good. Emma, with her quirky sense of humor and slightly obsessive nature, turned out to be quite the match for his cranky-cat personality. She constantly made him smile, and when she irritated him, she still made him smile.

In short, the woman rubbed up against him in the nicest way possible.

Of course, if she hadn't gotten him all sappy with images of all the things he planned to do to her tonight, he might have seen all this coming. But he walked into that room completely unprepared.

"Well, boy?" his father demanded.

Kyle stopped in the doorway and stared. "Well, what?'"

"Did you do it?"

Concerned what his father might actually be asking him, Kyle looked to Tully and Bear, both standing off in a corner. The look his brother gave him had the hairs on his neck standing up, and he started to feel angry before he even knew why.

"Did I do what, Daddy?"

"Did you send that little witch packing?"

Emma kept her head down, read her magazine, and ate her breakfast. She knew they were all watching her, she simply didn't know why. Had they never seen a half-Chinese woman before? Or maybe it was because she was the smallest adult woman in town. Whatever the reason, she didn't like it.

The fist slamming down on her table had Emma almost flying out of her chair. She looked up into a slightly familiar face. Maybe one of the nurses at the hospital? Then Emma realized the woman wore the black baseball cap, T-shirt and jeans that seemed to be the uniform for the town's sheriff's department, although the baseball cap was a tad too big for that head.

"Don't y'all have something else to do?"

It took Emma a moment to realize the woman wasn't speaking to her. Emma looked over her shoulder and stared at the three hard-looking females sitting in the booth behind her.

"We were only trying to be neighborly," one female said, and the other two gave high-pitched giggles that Emma found extremely disturbing.

"Go away, Mary Lou Reynolds, or I'll make you cry again."

Emma tried not to rear back as the female leaned over her chair slightly and gave a seriously unholy grin. It seemed wider than a normal smile.

"So, tell us, darlin'," she asked Emma. "Is it true what they say about Kyle Treharne? Is he the wild ride we've always heard? Or were you a little too tame for him?"

Nope. She didn't know what to say to such a strange and rude question. Emma didn't have confrontations. Hell, people barely noticed she breathed, much less got in her face. She could toss a spell, but the satisfaction would be fleeting. Especially if the townspeople decided to burn her at the stake or something.

So Emma merely stared and wished her Coven were around. They did all the ass-kicking when necessary, and Emma lied to the police. A very symbiotic relationship.

But as she watched a pepper shaker fly past her and slam right in the middle of the woman's forehead, she realized that sometimes help came from the strangest places.

Mary Lou screeched and grabbed her forehead while the other two women giggled hysterically.

"Now, listen up," the female deputy barked. "First off, never mess with the tourists. And second, don't ever talk about my brother again. Either one. Don't even breathe around them. Or they'll be finding parts of you around town for decades."

Interesting. Based on what Emma knew of the law, threatening bodily harm in front of witnesses... not really a good thing. *Of course, 'round here, phone stealin' is a hangin' offense.*

"Now get out of my sight."

The three women, after a little more glaring, skulked off. And it was definitely "skulky."

The deputy pulled out the chair and dropped into it. Literally. Kind of like a load of bricks, she sort of landed in the seat. "Sorry about that, darlin'. Some people just don't know any better."

"It's okay," Emma finally managed.

"My name is Katie Treharne-MacClancy. I'm Kyle and Tully's baby sister. You look cute in my way-too-big-for-you clothes, by the way."

Emma glanced down at the oversized white T-shirt and enormous blue boxer shorts she had on. Kyle had given her these when her sweat clothes suddenly went missing from his living room floor. "Thanks." She motioned to the now-empty chairs behind her. "And thanks for that."

"No problem. It's part of my job. Besides, I hate those bitches. Just downright mean. But all their kind is."

Emma blinked. Their kind? Funny, they all looked white to her.

"Lord, you sure are a little thing. I can see why Kyle's keeping you close."

Once again, not sure what to say, Emma gave a small shrug.

"Kind of shy, too, huh? I used to be shy. Sort of. Okay, not really." Katie grinned, and Emma saw Tully's grin with Kyle's eyes. A very nice mix on a woman.

"So," and Katie took a sausage off Emma's plate, the way Kyle had, "you in love with my big brother or what?"

Emma stared at the pretty woman. And she kept staring.

"Lord, girl. You look like a deer caught in headlights."

Emma cleared her throat. "Kyle and I barely know each other."

"'Round here that don't count for much. You'll find the people of Smithville make up their minds right quick. We see something and we just go for it. Like a cheetah after a zebra."

An interesting analogy that had the table of men next to them laughing.

Katie winked at the men and smiled at Emma. "Come on, darlin'. I'll show you around our fair town. You might find it very interesting."

Her appetite gone, Emma pushed her plate away. "I think I already do."

"You said they were evil."

Miss Sophie sighed. "You never listen, do you, Jack Treharne? I said, they worshipped the Dark Mothers. I did not say they were evil."

"There's a difference?"

"Trust me when I say there's a very big difference." Miss Sophie glanced at her sister. "All of you need to face it. Our Coven is gone. And every day, Addie and I get weaker."

"There are other Covens," Bear's momma, Gwen, cut in. "From good Southern families."

"Who?" Tully asked. "The hippies? You can stand that smell? 'Cause I can't."

"We could ask them to bathe," Miss Gwen offered hopefully, "and ask 'em not to wear that pawhatsit oil."

"Patchouli, Momma," Bear laughed. "It's called patchouli oil."

"Well," Kyle's daddy groused, "they gotta be better than these devil worshippers."

Finally Miss Adelaide slammed her hand down. "None of you are listening. This isn't up for debate. This isn't something we can go off and think about for ten years while you all fight for territory and a hunk of zebra carcass. Times have changed, and this town must change with it if it hopes to stay the same. There's evil at our borders, and it will get in. This Coven, they could be our only hope."

Kyle sighed. "I've seen Emma…protect herself. She's powerful, but I don't think she's as powerful as you seem to think she is, Miss Addie."

"On their own, they're powerful, Kyle." Miss Sophie rubbed her forehead, clearly tired. Twenty years ago she'd been spry and strong, but her age had caught up with her. "But it's the coven working as one that makes them the allies we need. Together they can protect this town from those covens you don't want anywhere near this place. Covens who make them seem downright cuddly."

"Why would some Yankees wanna stay here?" Jack pushed, clearly not willing to give up the fight on this. "Especially a bunch of New Yorkers."

Miss Addie snorted. "How could they resist all this Southern charm?"

"And the first Smithville settlers landed right here in 1610."

Emma frowned up at Katie. She had to frown up because the woman was huge. "In 1610? I thought the first U.S. settlers didn't land on Plymouth Rock until 1620 or so."

Katie shrugged. "We don't make a big deal of it, but we were here first."

With a nod, Katie started trudging back over the sand. "Come on. I'll take you over to the Smithville museum." She turned and faced Emma while walking backward. "I think there are some old photos there you'll find very interesting. Then we can go shopping. Tiffany's is having a sale."

"Smithville has a Tiffany's?"

"Sure. Don't you have one in New York?"

She fought the urge to say, "Yeah, but it's New York," because she knew how snobby that would sound. Instead she said, "Oh. Yeah."

Emma really didn't know what the hell was going on, but she couldn't shake Katie or the feeling Katie wanted to show her something. Needed her to understand something. Emma tried to hint at her government experiment theory, but Katie only stared at her.

Trying her best to keep up with the much taller woman's long strides, Emma studied her. Although beautiful, the woman still looked like she could lift a Hummer over her head for laughs. Emma had always thought Mac had a strong body, but Mac and Katie had one big difference.

Mac didn't make Emma nervous.

Not that she thought Katie would do anything, but the potential to do something lay right under the woman's skin. It didn't escape Emma, either, that she'd felt the same way when she met Kyle and Tully. Something raw and predatory she couldn't quite put her finger on. And the more she thought about it, the more she realized everyone in town had the same vibe flowing through them.

A quick jaunt back onto Main Street in Katie's truck, and they soon pulled up in front of the Smithville County Museum.

Like all the county buildings in Smithville, Emma now realized, the museum reeked of old money and powerful influence. Lots of marble and Italian tile. When Emma noticed they had a whole wing dedicated to Pollock, Monet, and Van Gogh—originals, no less—she knew she was way out of her league financially in this town. Although she did have a framed Monet poster on her hallway wall.

"Now, you could spend a couple of days really exploring this museum, but I thought I'd show you this wing. It's my favorite. It's all about the history and whatnot of my town."

Politely, even though convinced she'd be bored out of her mind, Emma walked down the hall, glancing at the extremely old pictures. Some clearly dating back to the late 1800s. As her eyes passed each photo, she suddenly stopped and took a step back, staring intently at the shot of six women dressed in ceremonial robes. She recognized the emblem on their clothes from one of her history of witchcraft books. An old, powerful coven, they worshipped Artemis mostly, disappearing around 1892 or so. Except the photo was dated 1905.

Yet even that wasn't what caught Emma's interest. It was the big lion pride asleep in the background. Emma leaned in closer to see if they had superimposed the images or something. Then she realized one of the male lions had his tail wrapped around one of the witch's ankles... and the witch didn't seem to mind.

Emma, heart slamming against her rib cage, took several steps over to another photo, dated 1958. She recognized Miss Sophie and Miss Adelaide immediately. Extremely young and not too bad-looking, they sat on the beach with their coven as well as two male lions, a cheetah, a leopard and a hyena. Not surprisingly, the hyena had his head in Miss Adelaide's lap, while one of the lions rested his majestic head on Miss Sophie's shoulder.

Then it hit her, like a shovel to the back of the head. Pirate dog.

That wolf in Kyle's picture had been posing. He'd probably been saying "cheese" too.

"Witches aren't the only ones who must be silent, Emma." Katie stood next to Emma now, speaking quietly. "Secrets are what keep this town safe."

"Then why are you telling me?"

"You know why, Emma."

Without another word, Emma turned and headed for the exit.

"Emma, wait."

She barely heard Katie's voice through the screaming in her head. Suddenly everything made sense. Every growl, purr, snarl... and hiss.

It also explained why Kyle could traipse in and out of her dreams so damn easily.

Emma stormed out of the museum and headed blindly down the street. She would have kept going too, straight back to Long Island, if that hand hadn't grabbed hold of her arm and swung her around.

"Hello, pretty little Emma." The creepy heifer from the diner. "Don't run off. We only want to talk."

With a roll of her eyes, Emma snatched her arm back and marched off. But fingers grabbed at her again.

Emma didn't even think about it, she spun around and let a spell fly, realizing too late that the one grabbing her arm had been Katie. In horror, she watched Katie fly back and slam into the store front windows of a Gucci store.

Glass exploded out and sprayed across the sidewalk. Some of the people on the street ducked to avoid the spray, but none of them ran. None of them screamed. They only waited until the glass settled, and then they all turned and stared at Emma.

It was the snarling, though... the snarling and the growling and the palpitating anger swirling around her that convinced Emma she'd just made a very bad mistake.

"I'll tell her the truth tonight. I was planning to anyway. And then she and her Coven can decide."

His father threw his hands up in exasperation. "Tell them who we are before we find out if they're staying? Have you lost your mind?"

"She won't say anything."

"How do you know? You barely know this woman."

"I know her enough."

"Have you marked her, Kyle?" Miss Gwen asked softly.

"No. I won't do that until she knows the truth. Until I know it's what she wants."

"You're a fool, boy," his father snapped. "Risking this town and your kin on this one woman."

"Just like you did when you were chasing after my momma," Tully murmured.

"That's not the same."

"It's not? Some Smith Packs were ready to kill her for getting involved with you. A cat. Lord knows, I wasn't happy. My momma risked her life to be with you, old man. And don't you ever forget it."

Kyle's father finally calmed down, looking sufficiently chastised by Tully. A few factions of the Smith Packs were notoriously unstable. So although Tully's momma wasn't a Smith by blood, she still had one of Buck Smith's sons. A meaner Alpha bastard few of them knew. He'd threatened more than once to take Tully from her when he found out Jack and Millie were mated and, even more appalling, married. But the town had protected them. No matter the infighting, the town always protected its own.

"Why don't you go get her, Kyle," Miss Gwen said softly. "Get her and when you're ready, tell her the truth. We'll decide what to do from there."

Kyle nodded. "Yes'm."

Walking toward the door, Tully behind him, Kyle heard Miss Gwen snap, "And, Jack Treharne, why don't you take your ornery ass home. Maybe that female of yours can calm you down!"

Kyle and Tully had enough respect for their father not to start laughing until they walked outside.

Emma backed up as they moved toward her. They'd ... changed, going from human to predator in about sixty seconds or so, shaking off designer clothes while jewelry snapped off wrists and necks and littered the ground.

No, these weren't some cursed "were-animals" or a crazy government experiment. These were a perfectly blended hybrid of human and animal created by nature.

Created by the gods. And protected by them.

I am so screwed.

Looking for any way out of this that didn't involve her killing anyone or getting herself killed, Emma threw up a mystical wall between herself and the animals. They briefly stopped. Not because they walked into it, but because they could sense it. A male lion with a huge mane raised his paw and tapped at the wall. But when his paw slid right through, he followed.

Again the animals moved on her, and again Emma stumbled back, now getting desperate, especially when that lion roared, the sound echoing for miles. But before he could take the next few feet to reach her, three hyenas tried to go around him and get to her first.

The lion snarled and swatted at two of them, knocking them back. Another male lion threw its big body against the third, sending it rolling into the middle of the street. But the hyenas righted themselves quickly and tried for her again. The lions slammed them back, unwilling, it seemed, to give up their prize. Several female lions joined the fray, as did a few tigers.

It turned ugly fast, and Emma stared in shock as the animals tore into each other, the lions standing in front of her. She knew they weren't protecting *her* as much as they were protecting their dinner.

Before she could think about running or doing anything, for that matter, a hand slapped over her mouth and dragged her back around a corner.

"I swear, Lucchesi. I leave you alone for two seconds and you get into all sorts of shit."

Emma almost dropped from relief at hearing that familiar voice whispering in her ear. She turned and threw her arms around strong shoulders.

"I've never been so glad to see you."

Mackenzie Marshall looked down into Emma's face and shook her head. "First you started that pit fight in hell, and now this."

"I think they're arguing over which bits of me they get."

"They're gettin' nothing. Let's go." Mac took her hand and proceeded to pull her toward the waiting SUV the Coven had rented, but the locals realized she'd left and came after her, moving around that corner like a combat unit.

At that moment, Jamie stepped out of the SUV, the expression on her pretty face making it crystal clear she'd tear the town apart to protect her Coven. Emma had to move fast. She stepped in front of Jamie and took her hand, ripping the power from her high priestess. The essence of it tore through Emma's body, shocking her with the richness of it. No wonder Jamie never seemed to have a moment of doubt about the path she'd chosen. When you wielded that much power, you didn't question a damn thing.

Jamie's knees buckled, and Mac caught hold of her. "Emma!"

"Trust me," Emma begged as she raised her free hand, fingertips up and palm flat. She aimed at the street in front of them, imagining herself grabbing hold of the Main Street asphalt the way she might grab a sheet on a bed and yanking it up and off.

The hard concrete heaved and, like an ocean wave, raised up nearly twenty feet high ... and froze. It even arced over like a wave.

"Holy shit," Mac muttered as she handed Jamie off to Kendall, who shoved her into the front passenger seat of the vehicle.

Emma started to follow Kenny into the backseat but stopped when she saw a tiger leap up onto the concrete ... and over, heading straight for Mackenzie.

"Mac!"

Mac turned, her fist already swinging wide and slamming into the tiger's jaw. The added fire spell really kicked it up a notch, though, knocking the animal back across the street.

"Time to run away," Mac yelped, jumping into the driver's seat while Emma slammed her door shut. "Hold on." Putting the vehicle in reverse, Mac looked over her shoulder and hit the gas.

"Here, hon. Drink this." Seneca put a cold bottle of apple juice in Emma's hand, knowing what she'd done had drained her. Emma gave her a grateful smile.

"You okay?" Kendall gruffly asked.

"Um—" She didn't have a chance to answer as Mac suddenly spun the car around, causing all of them to scream and grab hold of armrests or seat belts. Then Mac took off down the highway.

Mac glanced at her cousin, reached over, and slapped her face. Hard. "Wake up, cuz."

Jamie opened one eye and glared at Mac. "Don't. Hit. Me." She reached up and rubbed her temples, then took the bottle of juice Sen offered her before glaring at Emma. "And what the fuck were you thinking?"

"I had to do something. You had that look in your eye. That 'I'm going to destroy this entire town for my own amusement' look. But they were only reacting to something I did." Something she knew Kyle would never forgive her for.

Jamie didn't argue, which meant Emma had been right. "Whatever. Are you okay?"

Emma sipped her juice and shrugged. "I've been better. How did you guys find me, anyway?"

"We didn't," Mac answered. "It was more like we stumbled upon you. We had just turned onto that street when we saw you tossing the residents around."

Emma closed her eyes in horror. "Don't remind me."

"Don't sweat it, sweetie," Jamie said softly. Emma gave her high priestess two more minutes before she passed out cold from exhaustion. "We'll figure it out. Then we can decide if we want to wipe this town and all these freak people from the face of the earth."

"That's lovely, Jamie," Kenny sighed. "Reminds me of 'We Are the World'."

"I'm sure she didn't mean it," Seneca chimed in.

"Giggles doesn't think you mean it."

Sen slapped Kenny's arm. "Stop calling me Giggles."

Grateful to have her bickering Coven with her, Emma finished her juice and stared out the window as the town of Smithville whizzed by and out of her life forever.

THIRTEEN

Everyone thought Jamie had fallen asleep again until she suddenly grabbed hold of the emergency brake and yanked it up. The SUV spun in a tight circle, coming to an abrupt halt right beside a tree. A few more feet and they would have been wrapped around that tree.

Mac gripped the steering wheel and her emotions... barely. "Have you lost your mind?"

"Don't you hear it?"

Mac glared at her cousin. "Hear what?"

"Them. They're calling for us."

And before any of them could ask who "them" might be, Jamie had already pushed open the passenger door, and stumbled out of the vehicle.

"Where the hell is she going?"

They all unbuckled their seat belts and followed, watching as Jamie tripped and stumbled through the woods, heading to who knew where but moving incredibly fast for someone who should be weak if not completely passed out.

"Jamie, wait!" But it was as if she couldn't hear them, moving through the trees until she went over a ridge and they lost sight of her.

"God," Mac muttered, running up the ridge after her cousin but stopping suddenly at the top, Seneca and Kenny nearly colliding with her.

Emma made it up the ridge last, standing in mute shock for several long seconds before following her Coven down to where Jamie stood.

A graveyard. Their high priestess stood in the middle of a graveyard, powerful magick emanating from the land and out into the trees, the grass, the flowers. It hung off limbs like icicles and dusted the ground like snow. Emma had never seen so much concentrated energy in one place before. It almost blinded her.

Even the few seconds Jamie let the power wrap around her had rebuilt the energy she'd lost when Emma snatched it from her, explaining the sudden burst of strength and speed.

"This...this is amazing." Emma couldn't stop staring. A nonwitch wouldn't see anything except a well-tended but very old graveyard. The Coven, however, saw so much more. Especially Jamie.

"It comes from their bones," Jamie, now back at full strength, offered as explanation. "They die, are buried, and the magick that is inside them naturally, returns to the land."

Mac glanced at Emma and back at her cousin. "How the hell do you know that?"

"They told me."

Emma saw them. The ones who had come before them. The witches who'd protected the land and the people over the last four hundred years. And to be quite honest, they didn't look real happy to see Emma's Coven.

"Should we run away?" Emma asked carefully.

"Why?"

Only Jamie would ask that. Only Jamie wouldn't be freaked out by a crapload of dead witches standing around staring at them.

"We won't hurt you," one of them said. "We've come to help you understand."

Jamie sort of wandered away, touching leaves and tree limbs, playing with the magick in front of her. So Mac asked the questions. "Understand what?"

"Why you've been brought here."

"We didn't open that doorway, did we? We didn't conjure the thing that tried to kill Emma."

The apparition, a plain, dark-haired woman, smiled, but it wasn't remotely friendly. "Oh, but you did open that doorway. As usual, you ladies play where you have no place. But the doorway you opened allowed darker forces—darker than you, that is—to bring forth that unholy thing to terrorize our town. He had to stop Emma so she couldn't close the door. Others like that one were headed this way."

"Okay," Mac said calmly, "we screwed up. It's happened before, it'll happen again. What do you want from us?"

It moved around Mac, the other visions standing back and watching. Preventing the Coven from leaving. "It's not want, my dears. It's need. We need you to stay. We need you to protect our town."

Kenny scratched her head. "You're dead. What do you care?"

And the subtle award goes to...

"When we all came here, we had nothing. Nothing real. Our families had shunned us, our neighbors had tried to kill many of us. When we got here ... everything changed."

Another apparition with long blonde curls, who looked very much like Sophie and Adelaide, stepped forward. "We have families here now. Children, grandchildren, great grandchildren. We need them protected from those who would choose to take their power and use it. Who would expose them for their own selfish needs."

"Did you have no daughters, no sons who could take your place?"

Sophie and Addie's sister grinned. "The power of the animal always rules. Every child we bred went on to be a shifter; the only magick they wield is the ability to change from human to animal."

Jamie turned, her eyes nailing them all with one look, and Emma watched a few of the other witches move away from them. "So what's your offer? What do you want from us?"

"Simple. You give up everything to get everything. All this power can be yours, if you're not afraid to take a chance."

A cold smile on her face, Jamie said, "But we have to stay. We have to make this our home."

The dark-haired one nodded. "That's the price you pay. It's a choice you'll have to make. One we all had to make."

"Any regrets?"

"For some. Not for all. But that's for each witch to decide."

"But you don't want us here."

"No. You're not our first choice...but you're our only choice. Our only choice if we want to protect this town."

"We're not warriors," Emma admitted.

"We don't need warriors. The town is filled with them. We need witches not afraid to call on the darker powers. Who aren't afraid to kill if it becomes necessary."

Jamie blinked and glanced around. "Why is everyone looking at me?"

"You've been to hell, sisters," the blonde reminded them. "And they've spit you out again. That says much to us."

"It wasn't like that," Sen stated suddenly. And when everyone looked at her, she shrugged. "Well, it wasn't. They were real nice about it. They just asked us not to come back."

"Ever," Mac added. "They specified ever."

The apparition spoke again. "They'll come to you tonight. With an offer. You'll have to decide what you want and what you're willing to lose."

"And if we choose no?" Emma asked, always needing to know the options and the potential outcome.

"Then you go back to your lives."

"But if we stay?" Jamie tilted her head to the side, staring at the apparitions before her with absolutely no fear. "Then what?"

"Only you can decide that, sister."

Another apparition stepped forward, her eyes watching the forest. "They're coming for you. Not to hurt you, but to take you back into town. So they can give you the offer."

"Choose wisely, sisters. There will be no going back."

Jamie gave a small smile. "There never is."

Like mist, they dissipated, and moments later a lioness stepped from the trees, her Pride with her. On the opposite side, wolves. Some hyenas. Some tigers. Even a couple of bears. They moved forward as one, surrounding the five of them and making it perfectly clear...

The Coven of the Darkest Night wouldn't be leaving Smithville anytime soon.

Kyle stared up at the immobile blacktop. When younger, he and Tully had surfed waves shaped like this during the summer.

"Well, Miss Addie and Miss Sophie were right." Tully stood next to him, also staring up. It had to be twenty feet high. Apparently it had taken no time for Emma and her Coven to completely destroy Main Street.

I knew I shouldn't have left her on her own.

Tully reached out to touch it, and Bear slapped his hand. "Don't touch it, you idiot."

Rolling his eyes, Tully stepped closer and touched the asphalt. "It's real, all right." And as he said the words, the ground beneath their feet began to shake and rumble. Quickly, they all stepped back onto the sidewalk and watched as the giant black wave shifted and relaxed and slid right back into place.

"Good Lord," Tully muttered.

Bear scratched the back of his neck. "I wouldn't quite say that."

Katie pushed up against Kyle's side. She'd stopped bleeding, and the cuts from the glass were already healing. She flatly refused to go to the hospital, so they'd drop her off at their momma's house and let her take care of Katie's wounds.

"I'm so sorry, Kyle." Katie's head rested on his shoulder. "I shouldn't have said anything, but I didn't understand why we wouldn't tell her the truth."

Tully growled. "It doesn't matter. She shouldn't have hurt you."

"It wasn't her fault. Really," Katie admitted. "She thought I was Mary Lou, which I do find a little insulting, but still . . . no fault of hers."

Mary Lou Reynolds. Hyena bitch.

Kyle put his arm around Katie's shoulders. "It's all right, Kit-Kat. We'll fix this." He looked at Bear. "Where are they?" He wanted to see Emma. If she never wanted to see him again, he needed to hear her say it.

"Probably already back on the main highway, heading toward the airport."

Tully shook his head. "I bet ya fifty bucks they're still here."

"What makes you say that?"

In answer, Tully walked out onto the street. It had already hardened back into place, like it had never. moved. "Because, Yogi, the female who controls this much power ain't walkin' away from this town anytime soon."

"Don't call me that," Bear snarled.

"Go home, Kyle," Tully suddenly said. He walked back over to them. "Drop off Katie and then go home."

"No way. I wanna see her."

Tully put his hand on Kyle's shoulder. Probably the only man, besides his father, whom Kyle would let that near important arteries. "You'll see her before the night's out. But you've gotta trust me, little brother."

"But—"

"You go over there now, and that Coven of hers will think they need to protect her from you. As much as I don't like your feline ass, I'd still hate to see my momma cry at your funeral. So let me handle this."

Kyle took his baseball cap off and ran his hand through his hair. As much as he hated to admit it, Tully was right. If he pushed now, he'd lose her forever. Humans didn't handle the pushing very well. Emma especially hated it.

"Fine. But call me later and let me know what's going on."

"I got ya covered." Tully winked in that really annoying way he had. "Just leave this to the big dog."

Bear walked by them, muttering, "You are the biggest idiot."

The Smithville Arms turned out to be nothing like they expected. It was in no way, shape, or form a "quaint" hotel owned by two little old ladies. It was a resort. An enormous resort with enormous rooms and suites in the main building and family-sized cabins scattered around the property near the beach. As usual, the Coven sent Seneca in to arrange their rooms, knowing she'd get them a good deal, and she did. Because who could do better than free?

A surprising turn of events, especially when they saw their free rooms for the night: a "cabin" that was twice the size of the two-story house Emma grew up in with her parents, four sisters, and two brothers. It boasted a professional-grade kitchen with a fully stocked refrigerator and freezer, living room with leather couches and chairs, giant-screen TV with full cable, high-speed Internet access, a sitting room, a gaming room, and a bedroom with personal bath for each of them.

When Emma saw it, she immediately noted it was a very good thing they were getting the joint for free, because the only one among them who could afford it was Kendall.

Of course, they still had a price to pay because the Coven couldn't exactly leave, either. Since they'd walked into the place, they'd had furry bodyguards surrounding the cabin. Eventually, as their dead sisters promised, a town representative showed up to make them an offer.

Tully.

He and Jamie, after sizing each other up like two gators at a water hole, took their discussion to the front porch, while the rest of them remained inside and indulged in the enormous spread of food Mac made and the Merlot Kenny discovered in the cabin's wine cellar. Yeah. The cabin had a wine cellar.

Bottle two, and Emma wasn't feeling much pain at this point. Just a vague sense of annoyance.

"You made too much food, Mac." They had enough left over to feed them for days.

"I couldn't resist. That kitchen makes me wet. I haven't been able to cook like that since I went on leave."

"What do you think they're talking about out there?" Kendall asked, her head resting against the back of the exquisitely made dining-table chairs.

"Talking? The way my cousin was checking him out, she's probably on her knees giving him a hummer."

"The bond you two have warms my heart," Kenny muttered.

Eventually Jamie came back inside alone, carrying an enormous leather-bound briefcase with her, and dumped it at Emma's feet. "Some light reading for you."

"Huh?"

"They're books. Financial records for this place." Jamie threw herself in a seat beside Emma. "That's the offer. The same offer they've given every coven for the last four hundred years."

"Which is?" Mac pushed.

"This place."

Kenny sneered. "The cabin?"

Jamie shook her head and couldn't keep the smile off her face. "The resort."

They all froze, staring at each other over the piles of half-eaten food.

"You can't be serious?" Kendall argued. "This place must earn a fortune."

"Emma will tell us after she looks at their books. Apparently they pass it down from coven to coven. The money we make will be ours. The only restriction is that we can't sell it to anyone from outside the town."

"And we'll need to stay?"

"And we'll need to stay. We use our powers to protect their borders, to keep whatever is trying to get in out, and basically handle all the mystical stuff."

"And what do we get from them?"

"Besides this place? The sacred space of our choosing, the freedom to worship as we wish, and their physical protection. Which, I'm guessing, is quite mighty."

Kenny sat up straight. "You can't seriously be considering this."

"Oh, yeah. I'm seriously considering it. But we go into this together or we don't go in at all."

Kenny's gray eyes looked away. "We all know you've got enough power to do this on your own. What do you need us for?"

"Without you guys I'm just a crazy witch on a power trip." Jamie shrugged. "You guys protect me from myself. You'll protect them. I can't do this without you. And believe it or not, I don't want to. We may not be best friends or anything, but...you're my Coven. My sisters. We either take this journey together or we don't take it at all."

Jamie grabbed the half-empty bottle of Merlot off the table and took a sip. "But we'll worry about that later. Tully and the rest of the jungle menagerie left for the night, so let's decide what we want to do tomorrow."

Reaching over, Jamie topped off Emma's glass. "Here, Em. Drink up."

Emma shook her head, feeling groggy and a little disoriented. "Nah. I think I had too much already."

"Go on," Jamie urged. "Live a little. What's one more glass?"

"What are you doing?" Mac questioned softly.

"Shut up," Jamie said lightly to her cousin before turning back to Emma. "I mean, if I were you, I'd need a drink. After what that deputy guy did."

Emma frowned. "What he did?"

"He used you, hon. He lied to you."

"Jamie," Mac warned, although Emma wasn't sure why, since nothing Jamie said wasn't true. Although at the moment, Emma wasn't sure why about a lot of things. She especially didn't know why Jamie hit her cousin in the head with a dinner roll.

"He did lie to me, didn't he?"

"He sure did." Jamie filled Emma's glass again. "And if I were you, I'd go over there and I'd tell him exactly what I'm thinking."

"You would?" Something didn't sound right, but as she downed that next glass of wine, Emma didn't care anymore.

"Oh, I totally would. And if you want, I'll drive you over there myself."

Mac shook her head. "How the hell do you know—?"

"Dog guy told me," Jamie snapped while grabbing up a set of keys. "Come on, Em. Let's go over there so you can give this guy a piece of your mind."

"Damn right," Emma snarled, pushing herself up and letting Jamie catch hold of her arm before she hit the floor. "I have a lot I wanna say to that guy Karl."

"Kyle."

"Whatever."

Kyle snarled around the slice of key lime pie he was trying to eat when the knock came again. He didn't want to see anyone tonight. Then he remembered—his family never knocked.

With a forkful of key lime still in his hand, he walked to the door and opened it. Emma stared up at him, her face angry and her eyes glazed. Behind her stood a black woman Kyle had never seen before. Pretty. Tall. And with the eyes of a predator. She sized Kyle up closely and, after several silent moments, grinned. "Emma's here to give you a piece of her mind." She pushed Emma toward him. "Good luck."

Then she walked off, got in the blue SUV she'd left running in front of his house, and drove off.

"Hey!" Emma reached up and shoved his shoulder. "I wanna talk to you, bub!" She stormed into the house and Kyle watched her. Her friends must have brought her extra clothes. She wore the cutest little shorts and a smallish T-shirt that hugged her breasts perfectly. Other than that, no shoes and no bag.

Kyle closed the door and turned to find Emma standing right in front of him.

She punched his chest with her small fist. "You lied to me, Karl Treharne!"

"It's Kyle."

"Did I say I was done talking? Huh?" While standing still, she somehow managed to stumble, bracing herself against his body.

Good Lord in heaven, the woman is drunk off her ass.

"Jamie said I should come over here and tell you exactly how I feel about things. So here I am."

What should Kyle think about a woman who would dump her drunken friend off on his doorstep in the middle of the night? Other than he would make sure she had whatever she needed for the rest of her life, because she brought him his Emma.

"And you're going to listen to what I have to say?"

"Yup."

"Good."

He held up his fork. "Wanna try?"

She dutifully opened her mouth and he worked hard not to moan out loud while he fed her the bite of his mother's key lime pie. She shrugged. "That's good." Then her expression darkened again. "Don't try to distract me!"

"Sorry. Go on."

She stormed into the middle of his living room. And stood there. For a while.

Kyle placed the fork on the side table. "Emma?"

"What?"

He scratched his head, desperately trying not to laugh. She had to be the most adorable drunk he'd ever seen.

"You have something to say?"

"Don't rush me, bub. I'll say it when I'm damn good and ready."

"Okay. You thirsty? Want something to drink?"

"No. I think those two ... or three bottles of wine I drank is enough."

"That seems like a lot, Emma."

"Well, Jamie kept pouring." She took a step to steady herself. "Okay. So what I want to say is ... *Where are you?*"

Where he'd been for the last five minutes. "Behind you."

Emma spun around and he barely caught her in time. "Stop moving around like that. Must be some damn animal thing." She pulled away from him. "Anyway, you're a liar, Kyle Treharne. Sure, I didn't tell you anything about my Coven, but that's my prerogative. You, however, should have told me about the freakness that is you. And about this town, which I knew was funky from the get-go. Nobody's that nice!"

"I know, Emma. I'm sorry."

"Don't you dare argue with me on this."

Kyle cleared his throat. "Of course not."

Taking Emma's hand, Kyle started walking.

"Where are we going?"

"We're going to put you to bed, darlin'. Before you hit the floor and break that pretty nose."

"I'm not drunk," she stated right as she walked into the living room wall. "Ow! Dammit! Stop moving the walls around."

Kyle lifted Emma into his arms. "Sorry about that. Totally my fault."

"Damn right it is."

She wrapped her arms around his neck and buried her face into his throat. "You smell good, Deputy."

He practically ran to his bedroom. He needed to get her to sleep soon. Especially with her licking his neck like a kitten. "You taste good, too."

Kyle practically threw her on the bed.

"What?" she demanded, looking so cute and sexy he didn't think he'd be able to keep his hands off her if she kept talking... or breathing.

"Nothing. Except you need to go to sleep now, darlin'. For the sake of my sanity."

"Okay." Fully dressed, she slipped under the covers and snuggled against the pillow. "I am a little tired."

Thank God. He knew he couldn't take much more.

"Stay with me, Kyle."

"Emma—"

"Please?" She wiggled a bit. "You can spoon me. Preferably naked, please."

"Okay. But maybe I should keep my clothes—"

"Naked!" she ordered.

With a sigh, Kyle stripped off his sweatpants and got into bed with her.

"Gimme arm," she slurred. He held his arm out and she wrapped it around her stomach. "Closer. Cock against butt, please."

"You're gonna kill me, Emma."

"In the morning that's a definite possibility. Right now I don't think I'm up to it."

Grinning, Kyle snuggled up close behind her, holding her tight.

"Is that you purring?" she asked.

"Actually, no. That's you, darlin'."

"Oh. I didn't know I could make sounds like that. Hey. Wait a minute. This thing isn't transm…transmit…trans-something, is it?"

"Transmittable? No. It's not. You have to be born this way."

"Are you born furry?"

Kyle kissed her ear to keep himself from laughing at her or being insulted. "Go to sleep, Emma. We'll talk in the morning."

"O—" She never finished the "kay" part since she'd already started snoring.

FOURTEEN

Emma opened her eyes and immediately closed them again. What cruel person would repeatedly stab a knife in her forehead like that? And had the sun moved closer to the Earth? Because that could be the only explanation for the damn thing being so bright.

Soft lips brushed against the back of her neck. A strong hand gently kneaded her breast.

That better be Kyle or I'm going to lose my ever-loving mind.

"Kyle?"

He sort of hummed in answer and she tried opening her eyes again. "Why am I naked?"

Kyle had one arm around her waist, his hand resting against her hip, and he brushed his fingers back and forth over the area, making Emma pretty tingly.

"You woke up in the middle of the night 'cause all that wine caught up with you. Unfortunately you kind of missed the toilet." She cringed. "I cleaned everything up, brushed your teeth, then gave us a nice shower. No point in putting your clothes back on after that."

"Sorry about your bathroom."

"Don't worry about it, darlin'. Tully can't hold his liquor either, but he insists on drinking tequila every once in a while. I had to clean up after him for years so our parents didn't find out we were out partying."

"I'm so sorry about last night." She blamed Jamie for all of it. The woman kept filling up her glass with that over-priced wine, and Emma kept guzzling it.

"Don't apologize, darlin'. I'm so glad you came over. Whatever the reason."

Emma pushed Kyle's arms away and turned over to face him. She had to. His seriously hard cock digging into her back kept distracting her from just about everything.

"So you're a ... a ... whatever?"

Propping himself up on one elbow, he smiled at her. "Shifter. Yes. I can shift between human and animal. I come from a really long line of whatevers."

"What kind are you? I'm guessing 'cat' since Tully keeps calling you 'pussy'."

Kyle bit back his snarl. "Black leopard."

Emma cleared her throat, determined to face her fear. "Can I see?"

Watching her closely, Kyle asked, "Are you sure, darlin'?"

"Yeah. I'm sure."

Kyle shrugged and, as he had in her dream, only in reverse ... he shifted from man to cat.

A big-clawed, big-fanged cat.

Giving off a panicked squeal, Emma didn't even real-ize she'd covered her face with the sheet. "Go back! Go back!"

After she got herself under control, she peeked over the sheet. Kyle—human Kyle—lay right where he'd been, try-ing really hard not to laugh at her.

She shuddered a bit. "Well ... that was interesting."

"It's okay, Emma."

"No. It's not. I'm not usually this big a pus ... uh ... wimp."

"You'll get used to it."

She would? She'd be there long enough to get used to it? Apparently Kyle thought so, and, to her surprise, she wasn't inclined to argue with him about it.

"Do you like being this way?" she asked, trying not to obsess while in bed, naked, with a gorgeous male who wanted her.

"I can't imagine any other way to be. What about you? Do you like what you do?"

"Well, that's just a religious choice. It's not like I'm not human or anything."

"Really?" He raised an eyebrow. "Emma, I saw what y'all did to the street."

"That was more Jamie. I simply ripped her power from her to make it happen."

Kyle laughed and lay back against the bed. "Oh, is that *all* you did?"

"Don't make fun of me."

"I'm not. I'm just always fascinated by how you never see yourself the way the rest of us do."

Plucking at the sheet covering them both, she asked softly, "What do you see?"

"Me?" He reached over and grabbed her around the waist, pulling her onto his lap so she draped over him. "I see a hot little minx with no idea of the power she holds. A woman who can control lightning and turn it into a lethal weapon. A witch whose Coven scares my own father, who ain't ever been scared of a damn thing in his life." He pushed her hair off her face. "I see you, Emma. And I like what I see. A lot."

She blushed. No one had ever said anything like that to her before. Everyone else only saw the dependable, reliable, boring Emma. The Volvo. It seemed like Kyle saw the sporty, bright red, two-door convertible Audi she had buried underneath.

Kyle kissed her forehead. Trailed his lips over each eye and down her nose. His mouth neared her lips and she blurted out, "I have a headache."

Blinking, Kyle pulled back and looked at her. "Oh. Okay. I'm sorry."

She frowned at him in confusion, then she realized how he must have interpreted her statement. "No. No. I mean ... I have a headache." Emma swallowed back her insecurity. "When I have headaches I sometimes find that ... uh ... certain activities make them go away."

"Certain activities?"

"Yes. Activities normally done alone, but a partner could actually be a big help and a lot more fun."

After a brief moment, Kyle grinned. "You mean the activity of giving yourself carpal tunnel?"

"I told you I got that from typing."

"Sure you did, darlin'."

Kyle eased her onto her back, his body held tight against hers. "Now let's see if old Kyle can help you out with that little headache of yours."

She giggled. "You are such a good old boy."

"That I am, darlin'. That I am." He kissed his way down her body, paying special attention to all her favorite little hot spots. Licking and nipping here and there. Eventually his head disappeared under the white sheet, and she bit her lip. She had never seen anything sexier than that man slipping beneath the covers to go down on her.

Kyle's hot tongue swiped long and slow up her pussy, the tip teasing her clit. Oh, and she'd never felt anything better, either. Christ, the man had a way with his tongue. *Must be a cat thing.*

Emma reached back and gripped the headboard as Kyle took another long, luxurious swipe.

He said something against her skin and she panted out, "What?"

Tossing the sheet aside, Kyle looked up at her from her lap and answered, "You taste amazing."

She blushed again. "Thanks."

Big hands slipped under her ass and lifted her up a bit so his tongue had easier access. "Didn't you know that?" he asked between licks.

"Uh, not really."

"We'll have to fix that," he muttered while tossing her legs over his shoulders.

Emma's grip tightened on the headboard, her body rocking into his tongue, pushing against his face as he licked her pussy clean. Or at least tried. The more the man licked, the wetter she became.

She groaned loudly as Kyle pushed a finger inside her. His tongue concentrated on her clit, and another finger joined the first. They pushed in and out of her, then they pushed in hard, stroked inside her, while Kyle sucked her clit.

Emma screamed out her orgasm, her hands releasing the headboard and grabbing onto the fitted sheet under her. Kyle didn't stop, either. He kept nursing at her, stretching her orgasm out until she thought she might literally die from the pleasure of it.

Then suddenly Kyle was over her, his mouth clamping down on hers. She tasted herself and Kyle, his tongue desperately sweeping inside her mouth. Her legs were still on his shoulders, bent back against her. He reached into the night table drawer for a condom. He had it on and was inside her in less than six seconds. Or at least, that's how it felt.

His pace was hard and rough, just the way she liked it. As if he couldn't wait to fuck her. As if she, Emma Elizabeth

Lan Lucchesi, made him so crazy he lost control. The thought had her coming again, gasping into his mouth and wrapping her arms around his neck.

Without stopping his hard thrusts, he sat up and grabbed hold of her legs, stretching them out like a V. He fucked her hard, staring down at her the entire time, his fingers tight around her ankles, most likely leaving bruises.

She didn't care. She loved all of it. Emma gave herself up to the sensations, loving the feel of Kyle's cock powering into her again and again.

Not knowing what else to do, Emma again grabbed the headboard and, unconsciously, licked her lips.

Something inside Kyle must have clicked with that one little move, and she saw his eyes change from human to cat in a split second. She also saw fangs when his lips pulled back over his teeth. And she could feel the tips of claws against her ankles where his fingers kept their tight grip.

Emma didn't care. Not at all. So she smiled and then she came. Hard. Kyle right behind her. The two of them cried out as the sensations pounded through them, passing from one to the other.

Kyle arched over her, his satisfied groans almost making her come again. Knowing she had the power to give him that kind of satisfaction the greatest aphrodisiac she'd ever known.

This time, instead of dropping on top of her, he dropped off to the side. Immediately his arm went around Emma and pulled her close.

It took them a while to get their breath back, but once they did Kyle asked, "How's your headache now, darlin'?"

Emma smiled, her lips dragging across his chest where he'd placed her head so she could rest. "Gone."

"Well, you just let me know anytime you need help with a headache. I'll be more than happy to help you out."

"Your selflessness knows no bounds, Deputy."

"This is very true. I'm all about the giving."

She snorted into his neck and ignored his mock gasp of indignation, deciding instead to go back to sleep.

Fifteen

"Guys?"

"Back here."

Emma walked through the living room and dining room of the cabin, into the kitchen, and right out the back door to the porch. Her Coven stood at the railing, staring out at the ocean and the waning moon above it.

Jamie glanced at her briefly before turning back. "Beautiful, huh?"

"Gorgeous."

"So?" Jamie smirked. "Have a good night?"

"Yup."

"Where is the fine deputy, anyway?"

"Out front. Talking to Tully. I guess Tully's here for our answer?"

"Probably."

Seneca grinned. "Did you guys spend all day together?"

"Yup."

"You guys have to see this man," Jamie informed them. "He's gorgeous."

Emma stood next to her high priestess. "Do you really think so?"

"Oh, yeah. I mean ... *gorgeous.*"

"I'm so glad you think he's gorgeous, Jamie. That means so much to me."

Jamie frowned. "Are you being sarcastic?"

"Very." Emma grabbed Jamie's upper arm, yanked her down, and proceeded to slap the back of her head.

"Hey! Hey!" Jamie pulled away and when Emma advanced on her, she grabbed hold of Seneca and held the much smaller woman up in front of her. "You wouldn't hit me while I'm holding Sen, would you?"

"Wait a second! How did I get in the middle of this?"

"Mac's way too big to grab."

"How could you leave me like that?" Emma demanded. "You got me drunk and you left me with a complete stranger."

"What are you talking about?" Jamie peeked around a struggling Sen. "You're crazy about the guy."

"I know that. But *you* don't know him. You're not supposed to get your friends drunk and leave them to the mercy of guys you don't know. Didn't you learn anything in college?"

"Look, I was just trying to help a sista out. If we left it up to you, you would have run back to Long Island. Besides, I gave him the Meacham once-over," she laughed.

Emma stalked toward her, but Jamie kept a tight grip on poor Seneca. As it was, Emma was only sort of angry to begin with, but when Jamie started imitating Sen's voice and begged, "Please don't hurt Jamie. She's weak and fragile," all Emma could do was laugh with the rest of her Coven.

"You're an idiot."

"I thought we established this long ago?" Jamie placed Sen on her feet.

"Never do that to me again," Emma warned as she leaned against the rail.

Mac turned to her cousin. "So what's the plan, cuz? Are we staying or going?"

"I don't want to live in the South," Kenny argued.

Jamie patted her shoulder. "I'm sure you'll get used to phrases like 'Down the road a piece' and 'What are y'all up to?'"

Kenny's head fell forward in defeat.

Putting her arm around her shoulders, Mac gave the woman a brief hug. "Come on, sweetie. It won't be that bad."

"All I'm saying is—Jews in the South. Bad idea, in my opinion."

Mac chuckled. "And when was the last time you were in a synagogue?"

"The day the rabbi told me to get out because I was pure evil. I swear, you ask one little question. But that's not the point. I don't think we belong here."

Jamie gave a harsh laugh. "Sweetie, I don't think we belong anywhere else. There's nowhere else in the world where we fit. And for once, we're not the biggest freaks, which is a nice change of pace."

Mac nodded. "Now there's a goal."

Kenny gave one last-ditch effort. "But our lives are in New York."

"This is true," Jamie agreed. "And what lives we have, huh? I could go back and be shot at some more, 'cause that's always fun. Mac can go back to risking her life dancing with flame, because I hope to bury my cousin before I'm forty. And, of course, we both get paid so well as civil servants. Sen can go back to her fun-filled waitress job and get her ass pinched by strange old men with Mafia connections. Emma could give up the prime bit of meat I dropped her off with last night to return to her exciting life as an accountant for divorce lawyers in Merrick. And, of course, there's you, who never leaves your house anyway."

"But I don't leave my house *in* New York."

Mac rubbed her eyes with the palms of her hands. "In or out, Ken? In or out? Make up your mind."

Kenny started to say something when she caught sight of Seneca grinning up at her. Her eyes narrowed.

"And," Jamie quickly added, "don't *not* do it to get even."

Ken gritted her teeth. "Fine. I'm in." Seneca squealed and threw her arms around Kenny's shoulders. "Hugging! I thought we discussed the hugging?"

Emma gently pulled Sen off Kendall and allowed her to put her arm around her shoulders instead.

Jamie nodded. "Then it's decided. We're in."

They fell silent and stared out at the beach, each lost in her own thought or worry or daydream. They remained silent and unmoving for so long, a small family of deer wandered by.

Mac sighed in wonder. "My God, guys. Look at the beauty of this place."

"The beauty of nature, ladies," Jamie added. "Enjoy the wonder that is the power of the gods."

They did. Until the deer suddenly scampered off and a zebra came charging out of the woods, three female lions hot on its hooves. Unfortunately for the zebra, it didn't realize they'd herded it right toward three other female lions. These were bigger and appeared more powerful. They came tearing out of trees on the opposite end of the beach and closed in on the defenseless animal. The Coven watched as the zebra made a wild turn, trying to outrun the lions, but it didn't stand a chance. One of the bigger ones slammed her paws into its rear flank, sending it tumbling forward. Another large one tackled the zebra, rolling with the white and black striped animal until she could get her maw around its throat. She turned over again and held the zebra in her jaws while hooves kicked out and the poor thing made pained whimpering sounds. Eventually its movements slowed down. It wasn't quite dead, though, when the lions took hold and started tearing it open so they could get to the good stuff inside.

The Coven watched in horror while the lions ate and fought over the carcass right in front of their porch. They watched until the big cats suddenly became aware of them, stopping their feeding frenzy to look up at the women, their gold fur-covered faces soaked in blood. The two groups stared at each other for nearly a minute.

Then one of the lions roared.

As one, Emma and her sisters screamed and charged back into the cabin, Mac and Jamie slamming the door behind them.

Panting and trying not to run back to New York in her bare feet, Emma glanced up and found Kyle and Tully leaning against the counter. The men had discovered the leftovers from Mac's meal the night before and had plates piled high with food they were busily devouring.

With those eyes only the residents of Smithville seemed to have, they stared at Emma's Coven, and the Coven stared back.

"I tell ya, little brother," Tully finally said as he headed off to the dining room with his food, "I'm feelin' safer already."

Emma only had a second to catch Kyle's wink before she had to slap her hand over Jamie's mouth to prevent the woman from finishing the spell that would turn Tully Smith into a poodle.

EPILOGUE

Five months later...

Shaking her head, Emma walked out of the inn and onto the porch. She couldn't take it anymore. The incessant fighting. The constant complaining. It was making her nuts.

"Couldn't take it anymore, huh?"

Emma glanced over at her Coven. They sat on the porch of the main building, Jamie and Kendall in chairs, Mac on the porch rail. Only Seneca remained inside, busy checking in a couple of good old boys who had Jamie practically squirming. Emma had to admit, she'd never—ever—seen so many hot guys in one place. Shifters were literally and figuratively a breed unto themselves.

Still, she knew she had the best of the bunch... even when he was being irritating.

Emma rolled her eyes as the snarling in the house became louder.

"You sure they aren't related?" Kendall asked. She motioned to Jamie and Mac. "They fight like these two."

"Some days I wonder." Bodies hit the screen door and Emma stepped aside seconds before a giant ball of snarling, snapping fur bounced out onto the porch and rolled down the steps.

Impassively, they all watched as Kyle and Tully tore into each other. Emma didn't even wince anymore. Their constant arguing, which led to bloodletting, had become as common to her as having a warm body next to her every night. Of course, she enjoyed one way more than the other.

When the pair disappeared into the woods, Emma let out a sigh. "I'm going home."

"Any plans for the night?" Jamie asked.

"Long hot shower and television. Kyle's huntin' tonight."

"Bet you never thought you'd hear yourself say that about a boyfriend, huh?"

Emma laughed. "I never thought I'd say anything about a boyfriend, period. Oh, by the way, there's a barbecue this weekend at Kyle's mother's house if you guys want to—"

As usual, they couldn't say no fast enough. They were never mean about it—even Kenny—they simply hadn't found their place in Smithville yet. Emma, knowing exactly how it felt not to belong, didn't push. She knew in their own time, these women would find their place. Besides, Seneca made up for the rest of them. Especially with the Smithville males. They absolutely *adored* her. In fact, Sen knew about the weekend barbecue before Kyle did.

Emma turned to go, but Sen's startled squeal from inside the inn had the women quickly moving toward the front door. Sen stumbled out, pushing the Coven back. A moment later, two enormous tigers—at least five hundred pounds each— came tearing out of the inn, down the porch stairs, and into the woods.

Emma put her arm around Sen's shoulder. "Are you okay?"

"I just have to get used to them...changing in the middle of the inn like that."

"They call it shifting," Jamie said with a smile, straddling the porch rail with her long legs.

"Well, whatever." Sen gave a brave smile. "I'll be fine. I just find all this so exciting!"

Kenny, her feet up on the porch rail as she relaxed back against the lounger, waited until Sen was stepping back into the inn. Then, an evil grin on her face, she tossed out, "That shipment of gazelles came in earlier. Lots of little baby ones. Real ripe … and juicy."

Sen's hand slapped against the door frame. "I hate you," she hissed before storming back into the front lobby.

Jamie shook her head. "You're going back to hell, Ken. And this time … they'll keep you."

Laughing, Emma walked down the steps. "See you guys later."

"Night, Em," they called after her.

Heading toward her new car—a cherry red Jeep Cherokee Kyle fucked her in the night she bought it—Emma passed a male lion ambling out of the woods.

"Hi, Dr. Sahara!" she called out cheerfully.

He roared back in greeting and kept going. She'd stopped screaming and running at the sight of him nearly two months ago, which made her very proud.

Yeah, life in Smithville wasn't exactly normal, but she couldn't say it wasn't fun, either.

After beating Tully into the ground, Kyle made it home in record time. He'd planned to go hunting with Tully and his Pack, but he realized he'd rather go home and see his Emma. But she hadn't gotten back yet from the inn, so he climbed his favorite tree and lay out on one of the lower branches so he could lick the wounds Tully gave him.

That didn't take long and he was just drifting off to sleep when the shades in his bedroom opened up. It was dark now, and he could easily see inside his well-lit house. And he got the feeling Emma knew that.

Especially when she started to take her clothes off... slowly.

Lord, he absolutely loved that woman. True, all that witch stuff took some getting used to. Especially when she came home the last full moon bruised like she'd been in a fight. She wouldn't tell him what had happened and then never gave him a chance to force the issue. Instead she practically threw him on the dining room table and had her dirty, horny way with him. She was always so horny after "spellcasting," as she called it. Hungry and horny.

Whatever. It didn't matter. He loved it. Besides, Emma didn't flaunt that side of her life. It was simply part of her, and he loved it like he loved her. Of course, Kyle was on his own for Sunday church, but his momma had learned to let that go.

Funny thing was, Emma still hadn't "officially" moved in. She'd taken one of the houses on the resort property, yet she hadn't even unpacked the boxes she brought back from New York, where Kyle had met her less-than-friendly family. Instead she spent every night in his house and called it "home."

Must be some human thing. She kept saying they had to get to know each other better before moving in together. But Kyle knew all he needed to know. She smelled good. She tasted even better. And she made him laugh. The cat was content, and that's all the cat needed to know.

What he hadn't mentioned to her was that he'd slowly started moving her stuff into his house. She wanted to read the newspaper, and it took her a second to realize she'd turned on her own lamp on his end table by the couch. The drawers he gave her for clothes kept getting fuller. Same thing with her closet. And if she grabbed another book off the bookshelf and exclaimed, "Hey! I have this book," one more time... he was gonna laugh at her. And she really hated when he laughed at her.

Kyle watched as she worked her way down to her white lace bra and matching panties that hugged her ass like a tight pair of boy's shorts. He loved when she wore those. She turned her back to him and unlatched the front clasp, slowly pulling the bra off. *My shy little Emma*, he thought with a laugh that came out as a bark.

Her thumbs hooked into the top of her panties and she bent over to slowly lower them. Kyle groaned, enjoying every second of it. Then, without even glancing out the window, she headed off to the bathroom.

Kyle stood up and made a wild leap from the tree branch. He slammed against the side of his house, his claws digging into the wood. Reaching out, he latched hold of the windowsill, pulling himself over. Pushing his paw through the small opening between the window and the sill, Kyle forced the window open enough so he could wiggle his big body through it. Landing silently on the floor, he walked to the bathroom. He could hear the water running and smell Emma's scent mingling with the steam. Purring low, he nudged the door open with his muzzle and entered. He could see her on the other side of the glass door as she soaped her gorgeous little body, and his mouth watered.

The shower door opened out, and as leopard he had no thumbs, so he stood on his hind legs and slapped his front paws against the glass. She turned and looked at him.

"You want something, pretty kitty?"

He roared impatiently and scratched at the glass, leaving marks.

"Okay. Okay. Calm yourself." She laughed as she opened the door and he leaped inside. She stood directly under the spray while he wound his long body around her legs. He licked the back of her knees, and she giggled. "Stop that!"

With one last nuzzle against her thigh, Kyle shifted from cat to man.

She smiled up at him, and his hard cat heart melted while his hard-on doubled in size.

"I'm glad you're home," she said softly.

He pushed her hair out of her face. "Me, too, darlin'."

With a bar of soap and her soft hands, she started to clean him off. He closed his eyes and let her have her dirty way with him, enjoying it all. Until she took firm hold of his cock, and his knees almost gave out.

"Did that hurt?"

"What?" he gasped out as her hand ran down the length of him.

"Those rips you have on your arm from fighting with Tully."

Kyle glanced down and saw the scratches on his forearm.

He wouldn't exactly call them "rips," but he liked that she worried about him. Especially when stroking his cock while she worried.

"Those ain't nothin', darlin'." He leaned down and kissed her forehead, her cheek, then her neck. "Tully can't hurt me. Ain't no dog alive can hurt me."

He bit her neck and she groaned, her hand tightening on him. "He doesn't like to be called dog, ya know? He nearly ripped Jamie's head off when she called him Marmaduke again the other day."

"She keeps calling him that, and I am loving every minute of it," Kyle laughed.

Emma grinned, her small body leaning into his as he stroked his hands over her wet flesh.

"Look, darlin', I don't want you to worry about me and Tully. We just like to argue over stupid stuff. It's instinctual."

She giggled. "Cats and dogs?"

He unwrapped her hand from his cock and kneeled in front of her, kissing her lower stomach and loving that her breath rushed out in a gasp at his touch. "Yankees and Rebels," he whispered.

Her hands tightened in his hair. "You're never letting me forget that, are you," she moaned.

"Nope." He licked her deep, and her hips moved against his face. "Who'd have thought it, darlin'? Me and a Yankee. Momma and Daddy are still trying to deal with that."

"It could be worse," she sighed out while his hands kneaded her adorable little ass.

"Is that right?"

"Yeah. I could be a dog person."

Before she could say another word, he had her slammed up against the far shower wall, with her legs around his hips, his cock buried deep inside her. He stared down into her beautiful face and growled. "*Never* say that to me again."

Then Kyle proved what a cat lover Emma really was.

About the Author

Originally from Long Island, New York, *New York Times* and *USA Today* bestselling author Shelly Laurenston has resigned herself to West Coast living, which involves healthy food, mostly sunny days, and lots of guys not wearing shirts when they really should be. Shelly Laurenston is also *The New York Times* and *USA Today* bestselling author G.A. Aiken, creator of the Dragon Kin series. For more info on G.A.'s dangerously and arrogantly sexy dragons, check out her website at www.gaaiken.com.

About the Publisher

This book is published on behalf of the author by the Ethan Ellenberg Literary Agency.
https://ethanellenberg.com
Email: agent@ethanellenberg.com

CPSIA information can be obtained
at www.ICGtesting.com
Printed in the USA
BVHW012154291021
620344BV00013B/527

9 781680 681925